The Counterfeit President

David Huff

David Huff—Ephraim, UT
ISBN: 978-0-9988003-6-3
The Counterfeit President/David Huff
Digital distribution I David Huff, 2019.
Paperback I David Huff 2019

Dedication

This is dedicated to the people who still believe in truth and integrity and will fight for the right to be free.

"Here is the test to find whether your mission on earth is finished. If you're alive, it isn't." — Richard Bach

"The adventure of life is to learn. The purpose of life is to grow. The nature of life is to change. The challenge of life is to overcome. The essence of life is to care. The opportunity of life is to serve. The secret of life is to dare. The spice of life is to befriend. The beauty of life is to give." — William Arthur Ward

"The purpose of life is a life of purpose." — Robert Byrne

Other Books Written by the Author
Arizona Heat
Florida Heat
Nevada Heat
New Jersey Heat

The Medallion
The Valley of the Giants

Chapter I

It was 9:00 p.m. Central Standard Time. The meeting the President had in Chicago had gone extremely well with Mayor Hutchins and Governor Wade. He had gone there to dedicate a new federal building, which would house the joint task force that would deal with the gang issues in Chicago. It was a typical grip-and-grin and ribbon cutting, it was all a show of support for the federal agencies that were called in to assist in combating the gang wars and violence that had decimated the inner part of the city of Chicago for years. This new federal building was state of the art with the latest new electronic equipment boasting new satellite technology that was being used by the Drug Enforcement Agency (DEA), Federal Bureau of Investigation (FBI), and Department of Homeland Security's (DHS) Immigration and Customs Enforcement (ICE). With this new technology, all the intelligence agencies that had been brought in to fight the drug violence would have the capability to stay in touch with their parent organizations to keep them abreast of the latest changes going on in the international war on drugs.

The Chicago Police Department's anti-gang and anti-drug units would be housed inside the new building to help fight the gangs that were dealing and having the biggest influence in the city's drug world. This new approach would be used for the first time to close the gulf between the federal, state, and city lines of communications and show a more united front to deal with the plague of drug-related deaths and the collateral damage done by the gangs in Chicago. The goal

1

was to stop the gangs from killing each other and contain the damage in the pursuit of the American dollar and the turf war for new territory.

At first Chicago didn't want the federal government in their business of fighting the gangs and drugs in the city. But as the press continued to show the number of people dying from drug and gang related incidents as the gangs fought for control of the city, the cost of the fight was becoming too much to shoulder by themselves, they really couldn't refuse the help of the feds. The state and local police agencies were besieged by all the violence being perpetrated by the gangs as they slowly expanded their operations across the bigger parts of the city. The local police departments were under attack from all sides in their fight to stop the progression of the gangs as they fought for more territory and the right to sell their drugs to everybody living within the confines of their turf.

The turf war between the feds and the state law-enforcement agencies was part of the problem that the President was trying to stop. The state was afraid that the federal agencies would take over the duties and responsibilities of the local police departments. However, with the federal agencies coming in to aid in the battle being waged against the gangs, they brought in new money which would help in the fight. The state was almost bankrupt and the need to replenish and rebuild the city's deficit in fighting the war against the gangs was begrudgingly appreciated. With the new building came new people and their families, who would be living in the city, and were brought in to support the work that was to be carried out. Being in a financial jam, Chicago would never turn down the free money from the feds or the income from the personnel moving in. The President knew that the war on the gang and drug problem in the city and surrounding areas would have to depend on the federal government stepping in. This would be done by creating a pilot program to be used as a prototype by Chicago first with the hope that it could be used by the other states if it worked. This way the President would get credit even though it was the previous administration who had suggested that the state and the federal government get involved in fighting the war on drugs together.

As Air Force One lifted off the runway at O'Hare International Airport, each reporter was busy on-board compiling their reports, all the reporters were finishing their take on the festivities of the day, which included a press conference that was called after the ribbon-cutting ceremony. It was there the President said the federal government would be getting involved in setting up a national reporting system for drugs and other contraband database to help the local law-enforcement agencies fight the drug wars in their own areas of responsibility. This, of course, was met with mixed feelings by all the people listening.

Seeing the Air Force One 747 sitting under armed guard, especially at night, was a remarkable sight. The lights from the generators on each corner of the secure area cast an eerie glow, especially against the blue paint of the aircraft. Even on the ground, Air Force One looked intimidating to all around her. A little longer and faster than the normal 747 this aircraft was the crème de la crème of the Boeing series. The history of naming the President's plane Air Force One was started years ago. As most people know, Air Force One is the official air traffic control call sign for a United States Air Force aircraft that carries the President of the United States. The "Air Force One" call sign was created after a 1953 incident during which a Lockheed Constellation named Columbine II, carrying President Dwight D. Eisenhower, entered the same airspace as a commercial airline flight using the same call sign. In order to keep this from happening again, Air Force One officially became the designated call sign for the plane of the President of the United States.

As the President boarded Air Force One for the trip home he knew it would be a while before he would see Washington D.C. again and, if everything went right, maybe never again. When the big jet was finally airborne at its cruising altitude, the President walked down the aisle, past all of the reporters who were busily finishing up their reports, to his private room where he laid down to go to sleep. The press corps aboard the President's plane didn't understand why he hadn't brought his wife and kids with him on this trip, his reason for not bringing them along had been that one of the kids was running a fever and he thought it best for the first lady to stay home and take care of the children. Accepting it as truth, the press corps went about their jobs trying to get the latest story in before press release.

As the reporters finished their pieces for their news organizations, they hit "send" and then, closing their laptops, sat back in their seats and closed their eyes, trying to get some sleep before landing at Andrews Air Force Base. The President, who had already retired to his place aboard Air Force One, was resting comfortably in his bed. As usual, the Secret Service agents were in place outside his door, standing and watching the reporters and support personnel as they moved about the aircraft. Nobody was considered a threat to the President in any way, but for the Secret Service, protocol was protocol and the Secret Service was all about procedures in doing their jobs.

As the CNN reporter closed his computer laptop after sending his report, he closed his eyes and was starting to relax a little. At that moment, the Air Force One pilot in the cockpit received an alarm indicating a launch of a Surface-to-Air Missile (SAM) headed in their direction. The Radar Warning Receiver (RWR) on board the aircraft indicated it was in front of the aircraft and headed in their direction. The chaff dispensers automatically started pushing chaff out the sides of Air Force One upon the flight crew's immediate notification of the SAM launch. The pilot automatically pulled up on the yoke of the aircraft to fly higher, then banked right of the chaff bursts to confuse the missile's guidance system. This move created some panic for the passengers in the main section of Air Force One. Those who were not belted in were thrown around a bit, landing on top of one another.

By now everybody was awake and wondering what was going on in the cockpit of the aircraft. The copilot dialed his Identification Friend or Foe (IFF) squawk to 7600, alerting the radar operators at the Air Traffic Control (ATC) at the region control centers, who were monitoring Air Force One's flight path, the 7600-squawk indicated that the aircraft was under duress. The ATC operators on the ground would alert the U.S. Air Force at the Minneapolis Air National Guard base, which was located at the international airport, who were standing by on alert status waiting to launch their aircraft. With the first missile missing the target, a second SAM had been launched at Air Force One. This time the RWR picked up the SAM from behind. The pilot banked left as the chaff bursts went out of the aircraft again, pushing down on the yoke. The aircraft lurched as it headed down to the ground to get away from the second SAM.

This time the reporters were really in a mess. Some of them found their seats and were buckling in when the second escape maneuver took place. The others, who were not so fortunate in getting to their seats, were hurled around the cabin of the plane. With nothing to hang on to, they were thrown around like rag dolls from right to left and up and down, each receiving serious injuries for being in the wrong place at the wrong time. Two reporters from NBC were lying on the floor of the aircraft, not moving. One of them had a gash on the side of his head that was bleeding badly; the other had her leg broken at the knee with the bone protruding in the opposite direction of the normal bend. The ones that were buckled in were being yanked and pulled by the aircraft as it maneuvered to get away from the SAMs and were starting to show bruising from the seat belts that were holding them in place. However, they were still conscience of what was going on around them.

As Air Force One had started banking left and right, then climbing and diving, the pilot and copilot were fighting hard to keep the plane flying. With both at the controls with oxygen masks on to keep their heads clear, you could see sweat starting to form on the brows of their foreheads as they fought with the lumbering beast in the sky. Both pilots knew one more hard banking turn in either direction would be enough to rip the wings off the aircraft. The Boeing 747 aircraft was not built for this kind of aerobatics. Regaining altitude and once more in level flight, the RWR picked up another SAM launch, this time again coming up in front of the aircraft. The chaff pods were empty and, with no air defenses left for the aircraft, the pilots knew all they could do was another hard bank to the right, hoping it would be enough to throw the SAM off its tracking. The Air Force pilots flying the plane had flown F-15 fighter jets in the war with Iraq, understood all too well the lethality of the SAMs against a slower, bigger aircraft with little maneuverability to defend itself. The F-15 Eagles could outmaneuver the SAM systems, but Air Force One was built for command and control for the President to run the war, if necessary, with fighter protection against any kind of airborne threat. Flying through American airspace without a fighter escort, this sort of thing wasn't supposed to be happening.

As Air Force One was trying to evade the second SAM launch, the Secret Service agents guarding the President went into his sleeping quarters, grabbing him and half-carrying him down the aisle to the back of the aircraft to an escape capsule that would hold the President safe if Air Force One should have to crash. Reaching the capsule and placing the President into it, the agents sealed the President inside and headed back to the main part of the aircraft. With their major concern regarding the President now taken care of, the agents began trying to help the reporters and military personnel aboard Air Force One that were hurt from the violent maneuvering of the aircraft.

When the third SAM threat was picked up by the RWR aboard Air Force One, it showed that the SAM was coming directly at them. The pilots went into evasive mode again with the aircraft; however, the speed of the SAM was faster than the Air Force One pilots could maneuver the aircraft. The split timing of being able to turn the aircraft by the pilots to avoid the missile was all that stood between them and death. Again, pulling on the yoke and banking hard right, the plane did as its masters commanded, but the lock on from the SAM was a good one and the plane was hit in the wing by the number four engine.

The flight engineer aboard Air Force One had started transmitting a mayday call as soon as the RWR had picked up the first SAM threat. With the call from the ATC Region Control Center, the Minneapolis Air National Guard unit launched two F-16 fighter aircraft to try to find Air Force One. The ATCs would direct the aircraft towards Air Force One in an attempt to neutralize the threat of the SAM against the

President's plane. The lead fighter, using his airborne radar, found the aircraft as the ATCs on the ground were diverting other aircraft away from the threat, leaving a clear path for the F-16's to intercept Air Force One. The last thing the ATCs wanted was a midair collision involving the President's plane with another aircraft carrying people. With confirmation from the wingman, both pilots went into afterburner to intercept Air Force One. Both pilots saw the launching of the third SAM and even picked it up on their RWR screens and saw it hit the wing of Air Force One, causing the wing to buckle and send pieces of it into the fuselage of the plane. The holes created by the flying debris started sucking people through them due to the rapid deceleration of oxygen escaping from the airplane. At this point the pilot told the crew chief to launch the escape capsule holding the President. As the capsule left Air Force One, the President, looking through the front window of the capsule, could see the aircraft roll on its back and fly into the ground.

Losing part of its wing, Air Force One couldn't be controlled by the pilots any longer and started rolling onto its back and headed into a dive toward the ground. In the last seconds aboard the aircraft, both pilots realized they were about to die and started praying. Air Force One hit the ground at 300 knots, killing everybody aboard on impact. The once-majestic bird that was the symbol of the political free world was nothing more than a wounded bird that had died. The scar left on the earth from the impact was more long than wide and the burnt-out area showed the final resting place for the aircraft as it had come to a halt. Before returning to base, the two F-16 pilots circled the area of the crash site, flying a Barrier Combat Air Patrol (BARCAP) mission, sending out the location of the crash site via airborne communications to the ATCs until the ground units appeared.

The first priority at the crash site was to find the President and check to see if he was alive or dead. As they searched for the capsule that the President had been placed in, it was determined that it wasn't anywhere near the crash site and couldn't be found. Unable to find the capsule or the President, search teams, mainly made up of sheriff's deputies and first responders, were organized to find both.

The second priority was to contain the crash site and seal off the area, then look for any survivors. This was carried out by securing the area with security personnel, who at this point were more of the local law-enforcement people and volunteers who happened to see the crash that showed up to help. Once the area was contained and finding no survivors at the scene, a temporary morgue was set up near the crash site to handle the bodies of the crash victims. Nothing could be moved until the proper authorities were in place, and that wouldn't happen until morning when the National Transportation Safety Board (NTSB) was on site, along with the FBI and Secret Service, which would be in the next three hours. In the meantime, the Army National Guard was activated to take over the security of the crash site.

By now the medical crews had started appearing and were waiting to start the grim task of recovering the bodies and placing them into the makeshift morgue, and as they waited they began covering the bodies with white sheets and blankets. With the flashing lights on top of the ambulances and patrol cars, it looked like a scene from the first of the Die-Hard movies after the cavalry arrived.

The capsule was eventually located by its tracking signal, intact and empty, about a mile away from the crash site. All indications were that the President was still alive, which was the only good news that they had so far. With the President nowhere to be found around the capsule, all eyes were now focused on finding out just where he was. The capsule was picked up by a military helicopter and flown back to the crash site to be gone over with a "fine-tooth comb" and was kept under guard until further notice.

Chapter II

Walking around the crash site, the lead FBI agent, Samuel Hatfield, could see the remains of some of the crew and reporters, with each area marked with little yellow flags indicating human remains. Some of the parts that were strewn all over the site were full-sized torsos, which would be easy to identify, while the other bits and pieces would need medical examiners using DNA and other scientific methods to determine who they were. The burnt bodies would take the longest to name simply because there weren't any distinguishing marks that could be identified, except through dental records. These remains would wait till last until all the others were identified, only because the process of elimination would be used to narrow down the list of possible names not yet found.

Pieces of Air Force One were spread out over an area the size of two football fields, in each direction. The halogen lights were still being set up so that the NTSB workers could start gathering pieces of the wreckage together to determine the cause of the crash. The lights would be turned off once daylight was upon the scene. Until then the lights would be moved as needed to cover the most important areas of the crash. From his vantage point Sam could still see small fires burning and parts of the fuselage against the rising sun. The fire crews were the only ones allowed to be inside the crash site because they were trying to put out the fires that were still burning. They were also involved in looking for possible survivors, which at this point seemed fruitless. Sam couldn't help but feel sad for the loss of life for all involved, their dreams and plans no longer to be accomplished or concluded. The impact of the crash and the loss of life would have a long-term impact on their families and friends. The question of who would do something like this was now being asked and would be the hardest thing to answer. This question was now being looked at by all the intelligence agencies involved in finding out who did this and why. At this point the FBI would take over as the lead investigators and collect all the evidence found on site to build the case against the unknown assailants.

Helicopters from the military were flying around farther out from the crash site, using their searchlights to try to find the location of the President. Using the escape pod as a reference point to start from, they spread out in all directions, hoping they would find some kind of clue that would lead them to the President. Each helicopter was being tracked by personnel in the command post, who were plotting their routes on a map stuck to a plexiglass board. The plane crash occurred in a rural part of Minnesota, where farming was the main way of life for the people who lived out here in the sticks. As the news spread, more and more emergency medical equipment and personnel was being moved into the area, including reporters who were being awakened to the terrible news by their bosses and told to get out there and get the scoop of the century.

At this point, nothing could be confirmed or denied by the command post because no one knew the extent of the damage at the crash site. Morning would reveal all of it and that wouldn't occur for another two-and-a-half hours. Fortunately, the days were longer in the summer and sunrise would be early. Until then, all the reporters could do was speculate about what happened.

FBI Special Agent Sam Hatfield had been called from his office in Minneapolis to take charge of the security for the crash site until others would arrive to help. Taking a military helicopter to the site, he took over the investigation immediately upon touching down and walked into the command center. From there he directed the local law-enforcement agencies to set up a perimeter around the crash site and provide initial security to control access to the site.

By now the news reporters were starting to show up, along with their trucks with the antennas on top, to start reporting what they didn't know about and had no clue of, each wanting to be the first to say they really had no idea about what had happened at the crash site other than the obvious. They all were pressing the FBI personnel and anybody else that happened to be standing about, questioning them about what they thought had happened overnight, then reporting it as fact until some new information came out that would contradict what they had just reported. Unfortunately, this also fell under the purview of Sam Hatfield.

Sam, watching the reporters, knew eventually he would have to talk to them and dreaded it. To him, reporters were less than human beings. The common joke that Sam had heard was that some of the agents would rather have their sisters be hookers than reporters, their contention being that hookers were more respected than the reporters they had dealt with in the past. Sam never bought into that statement, although sometimes he felt it was close to the truth.

At this point, everything that had to do with the plane crash was considered top secret, on a need-to-know basis only. This would save Sam from having to say anything to the reporters until there was more to go on and someone else at a higher pay grade made the decision to talk about it. His job was to secure the site and set up a command post to oversee the cleanup.

By now other personnel from the federal agencies were starting to show up to back up the others already there, one of which was the NTSB, who had just landed near the command post, via helicopter, to receive a Situation Report (Sitrep) briefing from Sam. The lead NTSB investigator, who was in front of his team, motioned for his people to wait outside while he went inside the command post. Showing his credentials and sticking out his hand, he shook Sam's hand, "Hi, I'm Bill Thomas. What's happening that you can tell us?"

Sam cleared his throat, "All I know for sure is that Air Force One has crashed and there are no survivors as of yet. We really don't know what happened to bring it down. All we know is basically what you see. I'm sure this isn't your first rodeo and I'm glad you're here to start to figure it out. Please let me know if you turn anything up that is contrary to what is normal for this kind of thing."

"Not a problem; we'll keep you posted on what we find. Can we use the command post as ours until we get more of our personnel in here?"

"Yes, just don't get in the way of our people, if possible, as you do your jobs and, remember, this is considered top secret, leastwise until you can tell us what happened."

"Roger that and thanks."

With that, Bill started barking out orders to his team and, as they looked at the map of the area, the team was trying to figure out what the best course of action would be to start their jobs. Within fifteen minutes they all headed out the door of the command post, making their way with their cameras and gear to look over the crash site and to start looking for the black box that had been aboard Air Force One. This would provide a lot of answers to the questions that now needed answering.

By now the sun was coming up and the medical crews were anxious to get started on removing the bodies from the site. At this point another helicopter was starting to land near the command post. Sam, looked at it, it was black with no markings and immediately recognized it as one of the FBI's helicopters. As he stood there waiting to see who was aboard, the doors opened and three agents came out of it. At once Sam recognized one of the men as being from Washington D.C., the other two were his assistants. When the man walked up to Sam, Sam grabbed him by the arm and escorted him into the command post. As they entered the command post, the senior FBI agent asked, "Sam, what's going on?"

"Well, other than the obvious, we really don't have anything new to report, only that we found the escape capsule that the President was supposed to be in and that we haven't found him yet. There is a possibility that he could have survived the plane crash. As it stands, we have helicopters out searching for him right now. We just don't have enough information yet to draw any conclusions at this point."

"Is the area secured and has everybody been verified that needs to be here?"

"We are using the local LEOs (Law Enforcement Officers) right now for security of the site until the military gets here to take over. The NTSB is here and have started their work and are presently looking for the black box. I could use more agents on the ground to help with anything else that might come up."

"From the air I could see lots of meat wagons standing by."

"Yes, sir, downtime, I was waiting for the sun to come up to let them in to clear the area of the bodies. In the meantime, some of the LEOs have been placing yellow flags where the bodies and parts are lying."

After some thought the senior agent said, "I'll send you some more agents as soon as I can; go ahead and use these two until they arrive. Do you have a morgue set up somewhere around here?"

"Yes, sir, way in the back, away from the press, where the medical examiners can do their jobs quietly."

"Good, sounds as if you have thought of everything. Good work, son."

"Thank you, sir."

The senior agent left the command post, got back on board the helicopter and left the area. Once clear, Sam looked at the two agents, inquiring, "Is this your first rodeo?"

Both nodded yes, "What do you want us to do?"

"I need you two to keep your eyes open for anything that doesn't feel right, including anybody you think doesn't belong here. This site is considered top secret until we are told otherwise. Basically, walk around and look like you know what you're doing, and if you run into anything that doesn't feel right, come get me."

As the two agents left the command post, Sam thought to himself that he was glad for the help, even if it was from rookies. He felt with the extra agents he had better control of the situation. Sam called on the radio to the guard at the gate, where the ambulances were waiting, "Let them through and tell them where to take the bodies."

With that, the gruesome task of picking up the bodies began, with some of the medical personnel holding buckets to get the small parts of flesh and bones, bagging them and marking where they had found the body parts. The list of names that were aboard Air Force One had been faxed to the command post from the Secret Service so that the medical examiners would have a starting place to work with in identifying the bodies. The forensics teams from the FBI and Minnesota State Police were busy taking pictures of everything that had to do with the crash. Pieces of Air Force One were photographed and categorized to be identified in a hangar that would be used to reconstruct the aircraft. This was done to verify and confirm the cause of the crash. The smaller pieces buried in the crash site due to the impact would be the hardest to find, requiring the teams to use metal detectors to locate them. The second part of the forensics teams' responsibilities would be that of taking pictures where the little yellow flags were posted in reference to the plane's debris. All of these points would be computerized to show a graphic layout of the plane where she lay on the ground.

Search teams had already been out looking for the President before sunrise, using infrared sensors mounted in the helicopters as they canvassed the area where the escape capsule had been found. With the rising of the sun, people were now being used to search on the ground, using first responders and bloodhounds to cover the area. After finding the escape capsule the bloodhounds were able to pick up the scent of the President and were sent off in the direction he took to get away from the pod.

All told, the agencies involved with investigation and searching for the President now included the FBI, Secret Service, NTSB, Minnesota State Police, the local sheriff's department, U.S. Army, and, of course, the local first responders, who had been trained for dealing with tornadoes and earthquakes and things of that nature.

All were appreciated, provided that all of them didn't get in the way of each other, which was becoming harder as the sun started to rise. And as all of them worked on their part of the puzzle, they wanted to control the investigation. The infighting only erupted once between the NTSB and state police as they tripped over each other trying to get their part of the investigation done. After a few words between them the state police relinquished their part of the search until the NTSB was completed with their fact-finding portion of their investigation.

As the sun started to rise in the east, the crash site took on a more somber tone. The area around the crash site was burned and the hole in the ground from the impact of the plane hitting and sliding forward left a jagged scar on the earth. The farmer's field of grain would be considered a total loss, not just from the crash but also from the human and vehicle traffic going in and out of the field.

With the sunrise, more search teams were organized to find the pieces of the plane and body parts. NTSB would coordinate the search for the fragments of the airplane, while the medical personnel and EMTs would coordinate the search for the body parts. Each search was set up in quadrants and each of these was named alphabetically by GPS and topographical maps of the area.

The lookie loos were now starting to appear to see what had happened. These were people who had a morbid sense of curiosity about seeing the bodies and pieces of wreckage from the crash. Each of them was asked for identification and if they had seen anything pertaining to the crash. Once confirmed that they knew nothing important, they were sent away and their cameras and cell phones were confiscated, pending review of the pictures they had taken of the crash site. The news helicopters now fought for the air space around the crash site so they could get the pictures of the crash from the air. All the major news agencies were there now and were showing the video of the crash site to the world every two minutes, then having their news experts explain what their take was on what had happened adding more noise in a world of too much noise.

With the recovery at the crash site now in full swing and everybody doing their part of the investigation, finding the President now became top priority and all other resources were being ramped up to find him. They had an idea of where to look; however, nobody could understand why he hadn't been found yet.

Chapter III

Sam Hatfield had the escape capsule used by the President brought to the command center for security reasons and had a tarp placed over it to keep it concealed from the prying eyes of the reporters and others that were in the area, at least until the forensics teams could go over every inch of the capsule. Their job was to look for fingerprints and anything else that could prove useful in finding the President. Once the forensics teams had completed their preliminary checks, the capsule would be sent to Quantico, Virginia, for a more thorough inspection to confirm what the original forensics team had found at the crash site.

In protecting the President, finding the escape capsule and the parachute a mile away from the actual crash site was considered normal. If the escape capsule had landed at the same time and place where Air Force One had crashed, there would have been a strong possibility that the President would have died in the crash. The pilot of Air Force One had activated the launch sequence for the capsule just as the plane started to roll over into its final dive to the ground. By all accounts, the pilot in his final thoughts, knowing he was going to die, saved the President's life by performing one last action to save him.

All of the intelligence agencies were notified that Air Force One had crashed and that the President was still missing. Each agency was on high alert, using their resources in searching and doing their part to find the President, not knowing where to look but knowing they needed to be doing something. They were continually checking their sources all over the world and listening to the latest communications that might give them a clue as to where the President might be. Each organization had designated one person to be their representative that would work with the others in searching for the President.

The FBI had started doing the interviews with the two F-16 pilots that located the crash site from the air. It was decided that Air Force One had been taken out by a SAM similar to a SA-7 style of weapon. Based on the interviews, the information was sent to FBI headquarters and the ATC radar video was sent to Quantico to be reviewed by the senior staff to confirm the cause of the plane crash. Two days later NTSB was able to find the black box from Air Force One, which was sent to the FBI headquarters for review as well. Unofficially, the cause of the crash was determined to be a terrorist action. The final report would actually confirm that the downing of Air Force One was in fact a terrorist action, but that would take a few more days after looking at the evidence that had been collected.

The last few minutes of the Boeing aircraft trying to escape the SAMs would be indicated in the flight-control data that was recorded by the black box. The computer-generated video would show that three SAMs were launched at Air Force One and that the pilots' flying skills were able to defeat the first two SAMs, along with using electronic countermeasures. The flight engineers were amazed at the stress the aircraft was under, with the pilot jinking the aircraft to get away from the SAM threat. The pressure on the wings of the aircraft must have been something else, and yet the pilots were able to keep the plane flying. Air Force One was one tough bird that had done its job well in evading the first two SAMs. The third SAM was the kill shot for the aircraft.

The pilots were still trying to evade it when the engine was hit by the missile.

With this new information, the hunt was on to find the terrorists involved with the shooting down of Air Force One and the kidnapping of the President. The CIA and NSA were listening to the chatter over the communications network and the WIFI network, trying to get some information as to who was taking credit for shooting down the President's plane. The interesting thing was that nobody, including ISIS and Al-Qaeda, was claiming any part of it, leaving the Intel community wondering who had done this.

The FBI started investigating the backgrounds of all the people who had been aboard Air Force One, including the reporters and the ground crews that kept Air Force One operational for flying status. This time the background checks would be more thorough on everyone.

FAA had handed over to the different ATCs the video of Air Force One as it had flown through the different controlled airspace, with the time and date stamps included. The video would show that the flight path of Air Force One was considered normal according to their flight plan, with the typical handoffs being done properly. The main thing the FBI was interested in at this point was to learn when and where the SAMs were fired. The algorithms used to determine this would be where the FBI would start their search to find the evidence as to where the terrorists had launched the missiles. The FBI teams were backed up by the Army CID (Criminal Investigation Department), U.S. Air Force OSI (Office of Special Investigation), NCIS (Naval Criminal Investigative Service), and the Minnesota State Bureau of Investigation. They too were looking for anything that would indicate which terrorist group was involved in the act. From the FAA video it was figured out that two teams of terrorists were involved with the shooting down of Air Force One. Located five miles apart in a straight line, the first team fired the SAM from the front, failing to hit their target. The second team fired their SAM from behind, again missing the aircraft. The first team fired once more from the front, this time hitting their target. Through good detective work the NCIS team found one of the sites used by the terrorists, discovering tire tracks, footprints, and some cigarette butts on the ground, as well as the burn marks from the weapon being fired.

The cigarette butts and plaster molds of the footprints and tire tracks, along with some of the grass that had been burned from the blowback of the weapon used, were sent to the forensics laboratory in Virginia. Upon reviewing this evidence, they were able to figure out from the DNA found on the cigarette butts that the terrorists were from Somalia and that they were driving a late-model Ford van. Based on the footprints, the stature of the terrorists was determined to be short to medium height and weighing about 150 pounds. The other site was found not long after the first one was, and it had some of the same types of tire tracks and footprints. It was confirmed that their initial deductions were correct as to who they were dealing with. All this information, along with the evidence, was sent to the FBI forensics laboratory to be confirmed once more. The DNA would later confirm what had already been determined, which was the ethnicity and the country that the terrorists were from. All of this took some time, but with the President missing, the level of priority was high and would be expedited as quickly as possible to all the other Intel agencies.

Sam and his team of FBI agents were still at the crash site when he received the word that Air Force One had been shot down by terrorists. Sam and his team now concentrated their investigation on where the capsule had been found, this time looking for the telltale footprints and tire tracks. They cast moldings of everything that may or may not have had anything to do with the President being kidnapped and then shipped their findings to the FBI lab, once again. With this being a terrorist act, all the Department of Defense investigative agencies were now concentrating their resources worldwide to try and find the President. Again, nothing was left to chance; the President had to be found, no matter what.

After all the evidence had been evaluated, it was determined that the FBI and DOD would concentrate their investigation within the United States and that the CIA and NSA would concentrate their investigation overseas, as their resources were already in place.

Chapter IV

When the President was ejected from Air Force One, it came as more of a surprise than fear. As he watched through the little window of the escape capsule, he saw the belly of the plane as it flew below him. Watching the big jet roll over and dive into the ground was surreal and almost like what you would see in a movie. Seeing the wing break up into pieces as the SAM hit it, the President was surprised at how fragile Air Force One really was. In its appearance as it sat on the tarmac, it looked as if no one could hurt the aircraft, as big as it was. The latest technology was to make sure nothing happened to the plane. It was amazing to the President that something so small as a missile could destroy a big powerful plane like Air Force One with one shot.

As the capsule floated down by parachute to the ground, the ground came rushing up to meet it. Landing with a thud, the capsule was dragged for about ten yards before coming to rest in a farmer's wheat field in an upright position. Realizing he had landed, the President pulled the handle to open the capsule so that he could get out of it. Once landing, the signal beacon started transmitting an emergency signal to let the world know where he was. This signal would be picked up by aircraft in the area and by satellites in space. This way the capsule would be found in minimum time. As the capsule hit the ground, the President activated another transmitter in his coat pocket that sent another predetermined signal to yet another receiver that was being carried by the terrorist teams.

It was only a couple of minutes before the terrorists found the President, grabbed him, and forced him into the back of a van while he was being gagged and having a hood placed over his head. One of the terrorists got back into the driver's seat of the van, and the other two sat in the back with the President as they drove off. The van was now searching for the second team of terrorists to retrieve them, so they could leave together. When they found the second team, the van doors slid open. They loaded them quickly into the van and headed off toward the interstate to head back to Arizona.

Arizona was the easiest state to get into the United States from Mexico, and also the easiest to get out of the country. All the terrorists had to do was to pay money to the cartels to get aid to go across the border. The United States government wanted to put a wall on the border, but the public outcry was loud and long; therefore, getting congressional approval was slow and hard to get. The irony of it was with funding down for the Department of Justice (DOJ) and Department of Homeland Security (DHS) and with workforce being cut, the borders were open all along Texas, Arizona, New Mexico, and California, not only for drugs but also for terrorists. It seems the public didn't want to offend anybody for fear of hurting their feelings at the cost of men and women dying aboard Air Force One or, for that matter, anybody else killed in a terrorist action.

The terrorists were in the process of meeting their cartel contacts to get back into Mexico when they ran into mechanical problems with their van. Evidently, one of the drivers failed to check the transmission fluid before starting the last leg of their journey to Mexico. Leaving the van near Nogales, Arizona, they bought another van that was like the one they gave up. They left the old van and headed to the border. They were unable to destroy the van for fear of attracting attention to themselves. After waiting a couple of days, they slipped back into Nogales, Mexico, meeting their cartel contacts from Mexico and using one of the dirt roads that served both the drug mules and illegals as a thoroughfare between Mexico and Arizona. Getting into Nogales, Mexico, was easy, especially with a cartel escort, as they continued to drive their van to Porta Vallarta. There they sat and waited to board a steamer that had been contracted by the cartel. After passing through the Panama Canal it was a straight shot back to the Middle East, all the while keeping the President drugged and concealed with a hood over his head.

In 20 days of traveling by ship they made port in Libya, where they were taken to a terrorist training camp and kept until it was clear to drive to Iraq. The road to Iraq was hot and dusty and the President was sick and had lost a lot of weight by the time they had reached Baghdad. Once the President had been delivered to Iraq, the mission for the terrorists was over and they would be known throughout all the Middle East for the daring exploits of kidnapping the President of the United States of America and getting away with it. Once in Iraq the President was put into a jail cell in one of the old palaces used by Saddam Hussein. The President was to be a bargaining piece for the terrorists to use against America and their allies.

With all the forensic labs that belonged to the DOD and the FBI working overtime to figure out the clues left behind by the terrorists and then breaking down the DNA acquired from the saliva on the cigarette butts, they were able to figure out the location of the terrorists and that they were of Middle Eastern descent, probably not far from Saudi Arabia or Northern Africa.

The tire tracks were identified as belonging to a late-model Ford van being sold all over the America. Naming the van was the easy part in the equation. Finding it was the long pole in the tent for the intel agencies working the case. The Ford van was very popular throughout the United States and Mexico and because of this it became a problem to locate the specific van the terrorists had used in kidnapping the President.

Their first break came when the dealer who sold the terrorists the new van suspected something was wrong when they paid in cash and left their old van at the car dealership. One of the kids that was hired to clean up the old van for resale was going through the van, clearing out the garbage from inside. The owner of the dealership happened to be walking by when he saw the boy reading newspapers from inside the van. All the newspapers were from across the United States, starting in Minnesota, then Texas, and then Phoenix. The owner thought that it was interesting that the papers were from different parts of the country, all of which places dealt with Air Force One being destroyed and the President missing.

With the men buying the new van with cash and finding the newspapers from across the United States in the van that had been left behind, the dealer decided to call the local police about what he had found. He picked up the phone and called the police department: "I don't know if this is anything worth reporting, but I have a Ford van down here that was traded by some Middle Eastern men who paid cash for a new van."

The desk sergeant who took the call transferred the car dealer to the detectives' unit who, after listening to him as he retold his story, took his information and said they would be down in a couple of minutes to see for themselves and not to touch anything in the van and to keep people away from it. The detectives sent a squad car to the dealership to verify what the car dealer had said. The dealer met the police officers and showed them the van. After going through the van themselves, they called the detectives, who arrived shortly thereafter to see for themselves. Knowing this could be the van that had been posted on the nationwide BOLO (be on the lookout), the FBI was called in to take a look. When the FBI showed up, the local detectives escorted them to the van, telling them what the car dealer had told them.

The agents, looking at the van and at the APB (All-Points Bulletin) that had just been released, which had identified the type of van used by the terrorists to kidnap the President, realized their good fortune in seeing that very van parked in front of them. Calling the Phoenix office, they let the senior agent know what they had found there in Nogales. By now the local police forensics team was on site and setting up to go through the van and start getting fingerprints and whatever else they could find. Some of the trash they found inside the van was old coffee cups, soft-drink cans, and other foodstuffs left behind, in other words, a DNA bonanza to go through. The forensics team was known for working with the local federal agencies simply because of how small the federal agencies were in Nogales.

The forensics team was able to find fingerprints of some of the terrorists and DNA samples that named the terrorists as well. One of the DNA samples, along with a smudged fingerprint, belonged to the President. The fingerprints of the terrorists were found on the newspapers, inside the arm rests and on the steering wheel and the back of the rearview mirror. In short order, the FBI had positive proof that the President had been kidnapped and that it was terrorists that had come through Arizona to do it.

Sam Hatfield sat down as he started reading the report of the van being located with fingerprints and DNA all through the van. With the cleanup of Air Force One in progress and with the bodies in the morgue having been named by the medical examiners, this part of the investigation was starting to wrap up as far as the FBI was concerned. It was now up to the NTSB to finish their work and piece together the wreckage of Air Force One to finally confirm that it was shot down by a Surface-to-Air Missile.

Sam left for Nogales, Arizona, via Phoenix that day, arriving about midnight on the red eye flight out of Minneapolis, St. Paul. Most of the fingerprints had been identified in the preliminary report, which was waiting for Sam once he arrived. According to the report, the terrorists had been found as a faction based in Somalia, which had been barely heard of, but was considered more radical than ISIS and Al-Qaeda combined. Working hand in hand in training with ISIS, they had grown to be considered a major threat to neighboring countries, lacking the funding to venture anywhere else in the world. This group was known as Al-Shebiib Jihadist Fundamentalist Group based in East Africa. In 2010 it pledged allegiance to the militant Islamist organization, Al-Qaeda, which became part of ISIS. The group describes itself as waging jihad against "enemies of Islam" and is engaged in combat against any border nation next to Somalia that does not practice their brand of religion. This was the first time this terrorist group had stepped outside of Africa to take part in any terrorist action in other overseas countries.

The two local FBI agents assigned to the case met Sam at the airport in Nogales. After picking up Sam's luggage they all promptly got into their car and drove to the FBI office. After having read the synopsis of the report about the terrorist group on the flight down, the agents gave him a quick rundown on the rest of the report. Sam then asked, "Did you find anything else of value from the van?"

"We're tracking the van that was left behind to see where they bought it. We were hoping to find out how they were able to buy the van. We think there was someone else who had been here for a while with a driver's license who bought it. If we can find him, we may be able to get more information as to where they may be taking the President. As of yet, we have nothing to report, other than the fingerprints they left behind," the lead agent said.

"I'm surprised that the van wasn't burned to hide the fingerprints," the second agent added.

"They were probably in a hurry and thought it would attract too much attention to do so," Sam replied.

"Either way, it was a lucky break for us. Do you plan on following the trail of the van into Mexico?" The lead agent asked.

"Will it do any good to do so?" asked Sam.

"You never know. I know of a joint operation between the FBI in Phoenix and the Phoenix Police Department working with the Border Patrol that may be of help if you decide to go into Mexico," the lead agent said.

"Please continue," Sam replied.

"The lead agent is a guy by the name of Bertrand, who runs the task force in Phoenix. He has two other agents who work with him by name of Miguel and Lucas, who know the area of Mexico like the back of their hands. They would know where to look for the President, the terrorists, and the van if they are still in Mexico."

"Are they any good at what they do?"

"Do you remember the Monterey Cartel, that was taken out a few years back?"

"Yes, I remember something about that cartel going away. These two people did that all by themselves?" Thinking for a moment, Sam continued, "Can you call Bertrand and get his team down here?"

"They're on their way down now. We took a chance and called them earlier, thinking that you would want to meet them. We figured that they may be of help in tracking the President."

Sam looked surprised by the answer and smiled, "Is there anything else I need before I ask?"

Both of local agents laughed at his question as the lead agent said, "You got to try harder when you're not number one in the FBI."

They all chuckled at the remark and sat down to wait for Bertrand to show up with Miguel and Lucas. As they waited they drank their coffee and told war stories about Nogales and Minneapolis and the different drug wars going on. Thirty minutes later Bertrand showed up, and after parking their car all three men got out of their government vehicle. They were met by the lead agent, who introduced himself as Watkins and his partner as agent Guymon. From there Watkins introduced Sam Hatfield to Bertrand, Miguel, and Lucas, as the lead agent in charge of the investigation of the kidnapping of the President. After shaking hands all around they went into a small conference room. Making sure everybody had some coffee to drink, they sat down, waiting for the briefing to begin.

Watkins started off, "Glad you guys could make the trip safely." He then continued to say, "We found the van used by the terrorists to kidnap the President. It was left in Nogales just the other day at a dealership where they traded for another van. It seems they burned the transmission out of the old van on their way back to Mexico."

"I'm surprised they didn't destroy the old van before getting a new one; that's usually their way of distancing themselves from trouble," Bertrand said.

"To be honest, we are too. They must have been in a hurry and didn't want to attract any more attention to themselves," Watkins replied.

"I take it you got fingerprints and such from the van that was left behind?" Miguel asked.

"We did, and we found out the terrorists are from Somalia over in East Africa, and they are considered a splinter group that has started to grow. They are now in bed with ISIS and Al-Qaeda, trying to earn the respect of both groups."

"Sounds like they may have done that by kidnapping the President and shooting down Air Force One," Bertrand said.

"Kidnapping the President was a very sophisticated move on their part. We think they must have had some help here in the United States, and that's what we're trying to find out right now," Sam said.

"What do you want Miguel and Lucas to do?" asked Bertrand.

"We need them to follow the trail into Mexico and see if the President is still in this part of the world," Sam said.

"Anything else you need from them?" Bertrand inquired.

Sam thought for a moment before saying, "Shut down the network that was used to get the President out of our country."

Miguel looked at Lucas and then Bertrand. "We have permission to destroy the cartel that they used to get the President?"

"Yes, with prejudice, we need to send a message to the ones that did this. We want the others to think twice before they try it again."

"We can do that without leaving a trace," Lucas said.

"Good, then I suggest you start as soon as you can. I think if you find the new van, it will help you find the President," Sam said.

"Agreed. We will leave tonight, and we'll let you know what we find," Lucas said.

Bertrand looked at the two men, knowing that if anyone could find the President, they could. The real question at this point was, would they be in time to rescue him?

Finding the right place to enter Mexico was easy. All you had to do was follow the people headed into Mexico via the port entrance. Lucas and Miguel left early in the evening later that day crossing over into Nogales, Mexico, just as the night life was starting and all the people who were wanting to be part of the festivities were starting to head into the Mexican town. As usual, it was all lit up where the cantinas were, and the women were out in force trying to pick up the rich gringos, hoping to have them buy their drinks for them and anything else that might have interested them. Lucas and Miguel knew to find the President they needed to find the people who brought the terrorists back across the border.

Not knowing where to look first, they went to a known hangout, where the cartel men camped out drinking their beer, waiting for the next trip to go across the border. Sitting in the back of the cantina, they listened to the locals talk about their experiences of crossing the border with the mules and others looking for a better life in America. As the noise grew inside and outside from the music being played and with the crowds moving about the cantina, Miguel and Lucas could hardly distinguish what was being said. Miguel decided to go stand at the bar and see what he could pick up. As the alcohol flowed freely and the talk got louder and less guarded, Miguel listened to some of the men standing at the bar as they were drinking their beers. One of the men at the bar was complaining that moving people back and forth was getting harder, now that the Border Patrol was looking for some unknowns crossing over into Mexico. The man he had been talking to agreed, "I wish It had been me bringing the foreigners over because they pay good money to cross over."

His friend agreed with him, adding, "With the money that my friends have made, they have plenty for the beer and the women to spend it on now."

After hearing the conversation end, Miguel walked back to the table where his partner sat. He passed on to Lucas what he had heard the two men saying. Lucas looked at Miguel. "Did they say where they could be found?"

"They aren't in here," Miguel replied.

"Maybe we should sit tight and wait to follow them. Who knows, maybe they will lead us to them."

"Unless they go to another cantina to have more fun."

"We don't have much time to waste on waiting to find out. How about we go ask them instead?"

As both men moved towards the two men talking at the bar, one of the men saw them coming and took off for the door of the cantina. Miguel followed the man outside and caught up with him, pulling him into the alley, he grabbed him by the scruff of the neck, and slammed him up against the wall, pinning him there. With his other hand taking his pistol and pointing it between his eyes. "Do you know where we can find the people who were involved with the terrorists?"

Lucas took the second man outside as well, doing the same thing to him as Miguel did to the first man. The first started talking so fast that Miguel had to have him slow down to understand him. Slapping the man upside the head with his gun to get his attention, he asked him one more time, "Where can we find the men who helped the terrorists?'

"I think one of them is in the cantina down the street."

"What's the name of the cantina?"

"It's called Maria's Place."

"What does the man look like that helped the terrorists?"

"He is about my size and has no hair on his head."

"What's his name and who does he work for?"

"His name is Marcos Mendoza; he works for the Zeta Cartel."

When he finished asking the questions of the first man, Miguel let go of him. The man slid down the wall of the building till he landed on his backside. Lucas brought the other man over and set him on the ground as well. Both of the men were sitting there wondering what was going to happen next. Miguel and Lucas talked amongst themselves to verify that the information given to both of them was the same. Miguel looked at Lucas. "What did your guy tell you?"

"He said the man went by the name of Hector, claims he worked for the Monterey Cartel."

Miguel walked back over to the man he had talked to and asked, "What name did you say?"

"Marcos Mendoza; he works for the Zeta Cartel."

"That's what I thought you said. Care to try again?"

"Senor, it is the truth."

Pointing his gun at the man's head and pulling the hammer back on the gun, Miguel said, "Your friend says his name is Hector; which is it?"

By now the first man started to draw water between his legs and was trying to get away from the muzzle of the gun. Lucas was watching the other man to see if there was any reaction to his friend's imminent death. Not saying a word, he sat there watching his friend. Finally, the first man said, "Please, senor, I was mistaken; his name is Hector and he does work for the Monterey Cartel."

"How do I know you're telling the truth?"

The Counterfeit President

At this point Lucas said, "Miguel, just shoot him get it over with; besides, we have his friend here to show us the way."

The first man started to cry now, knowing his time was close at hand, and he started pleading for his life. Miguel asked him one more time, "What is the guy's name and who does he work for?"

Trying not to cry, he said, "Hector; he works for the Monterey Cartel."

Shooting the man in the leg, Miguel said, "You should have told us the truth the first time. It's less painful that way."

Lucas looked at the second man. "The only reason we don't shoot you is because you told us the truth. Now go help your friend; he looks as if he could use it."

The second man picked himself up from the ground and, pulling his friend's arm, helped him to his feet. They walked away as Miguel watched. Lucas said, "You must be getting soft. I thought you were going to kill him."

"Believe me when I say I wanted to."

Miguel and Lucas went to the cantina called Maria's Place and started looking around inside for Hector. Going to the back of the cantina and ordering two beers, they sat and watched the people inside. Once the beer had been delivered by the waitress, Lucas asked her, "Is Hector around tonight?"

Of course, the waitress asked why he wanted to know and, slipping her a fifty-dollar bill, Lucas said, "Give this to him and say we have a special need of his skills in the real near future." Giving her a twenty to deliver the message, she said, "I will see if he is here."

Moments later the waitress pointed out the man who was with her, while Lucas and Miguel, sitting in the back of the cantina, were drinking their beer. As the man made his way to the table, Lucas and Miguel pulled their guns and had them hiding under the table, pointed at the man. Sitting down in

37

the chair opposite them, the man asked, "What can I do for you two gentlemen?"

"Who are you?" Lucas asked.

"My name is Antonio, I work for Hector when he needs my services."

Lucas looked at Miguel, "Come on, Miguel. I don't like dealing with the middle man on something this important."

As the two of them stood up from the table to leave, Antonio said, "Please sit down, gentlemen. If this is the real thing, I will personally take you to Hector so that you can talk to him yourselves."

Lucas, looking at Miguel, nodded to him and they both sat down again. Antonio said, "Nowadays we have to be very careful because of all the stuff going on across the border. Now, how can Hector help you?"

"We would like to use your services in getting across the border into America. It seems that we have some stuff we would like to deliver to our friends on the other side."

"Why don't you give me your stuff and I will personally deliver it myself."

"A very kind and generous offer, but we would prefer to deliver it ourselves. Besides, how do we know we can trust you to take care of it properly?" Miguel asked.

Antonio laughed, "Well, senor, it must be important if you can't trust Antonio to take care of it for you."

Lucas and Miguel laughed with Antonio about his comment. "If everything goes right, we may need your setup later. But for now, we will handle all of it ourselves."

"What is it you would have us do for you, then?" Antonio asked.

"We want to deliver our goods across the border to our friends, who have a network to deliver our goods from there," Miguel replied.

"How is it you come by these goods, senores?"

"Well, let's just say some of the men hired by this company in Mexico City are hurting from the loss of their product, our gain, their loss, as one would say," Lucas said.

"May I ask who this company is?"

"It doesn't matter anymore. They won't be needing it where they are now. Can you help us or not?"

"Let me do some checking into what you have said, and I will get back to you."

"That won't do; we want to move it tonight before anybody knows that it's missing," Miguel said, getting up from the table.

Lucas was halfway out of his chair, too, when Antonio, looking at the two of them, laughed a little. "I see you are in a hurry to get to the other side. What's in it for me and my services?"

"What do you want for your services?" Lucas asked.

"It depends on what you are delivering and how much of it there is."

"How about two kilos for your trouble, with more to come later if all goes well on this trip?"

Antonio sat there for a moment, thinking, *"Two kilos with more promised sounds good. Better yet, if we kill these two after we get them to the border, we will have two kilos, plus all the rest of it."* Antonio smiled at the thought of getting rich quickly and having enough money to set up his own operation for delivering drugs across the border. He then asked, "When can you be ready for the trip?"

Antonio's offer to leave tonight surprised Lucas and Miguel and brought a smile to their faces as they replied, "We can leave in an hour once we get the goods to deliver."

"I will have my men pick you up right here in an hour, and I will personally take you across the border," Antonio said.

"You are too generous, senor, but as you wish," Lucas said.

As they left the cantina, they watched Antonio leave. Waiting a few minutes, they followed him back to his place. They waited outside the building where Antonio had entered until the lights were off inside. Opening the door carefully, they walked in, making sure to stay out of the doorway so their silhouettes didn't get made by the street light outside. They quietly made their way into the building and, as they looked around, they could hear voices coming from one of the offices in the corner of the building. Slowly making their way to the office, the conversation became clearer. They could tell the men were talking about the job for tonight of moving the two gringos across the border into America, taking their drugs and killing them so they could sell the drugs themselves. One of the men talking said, "Hector, what do we do with the bodies of the two gringos?"

Hector replied, "Pablo, don't you know by now, we bury them in the desert."

By now Lucas and Miguel realized that Antonio was Hector all along. Peering into the office window, they could tell there were three men in the room besides Hector. Lucas went to the other side of the window and made his way to the front door of the office. Miguel carefully checked out the building to make sure that the only people in there were him and Lucas, along with Hector and his crew. Checkout completed, Miguel showed back up and nodded to Lucas to let him know that all was clear in the building. By now Hector was ready to leave with his crew to go find Miguel and Lucas. As Hector made his way toward the door, Miguel and Lucas met him and his men and, pushing them back into the office, shot all three men before turning their guns on Hector. Hector, totally taken by surprise by the two Americans and seeing his team dead on the floor, raised his hands in the air and stood there, waiting to be shot by Miguel and Lucas.

"Where are the terrorists you helped across the border?" asked Miguel.

Hector was surprised, not expecting the question, he didn't know what to say. He stood there a moment, trying to come up with an answer. As he stood there thinking, he remembered how he had met the terrorists as he sat waiting for the signal from them to come guide them across the border in their van, smiling at how much money they were paying to have him guide the van across the desert to Nogales, Mexico. By now Miguel was getting tired of waiting for Hector to answer the question, and he fired his weapon at him, with the bullet hitting Hector in the leg. Hector went down, screaming in pain. Realizing he had been shot, he lay on the ground holding his leg, almost in tears from the pain.

"Miguel asked you a question, and it's not polite to not answer, Hector," Lucas said.

Hector knew he was in trouble, and if he wanted to live, he had better answer the question. He stammered at first, "Senor, what terrorists are you talking about?"

This time Lucas fired his weapon, sending the bullet into Hector's shoulder, missing the artery and going through the shoulder blade, breaking it into pieces.

Hector screamed again, this time lying on the floor completely as he yelled out, "All right, all right, I will tell you what you want to know. We moved the van and the people inside it three days ago across the border into Nogales and sent them on their way to Mexico City."

"Where were they headed once they got to Mexico City, and who were they supposed to meet there?"

Realizing Hector was starting to fade out from loss of blood, Lucas grabbed him by the shot-up shoulder, forcing him to cry out in pain, thereby regaining his consciousness. Hector then offered, "He was supposed to meet our bosses there to make their way to the coast to get aboard a ship to the Middle East."

"Who are your bosses in Mexico City?"

Hector, starting to realize he was not going to survive the night, looked at Miguel, who had asked the question, "The boss's name is Renaldo Hernandez."

"Where can we find him?" asked Lucas this time.

"He lives in a house in the city near the airport. It's easy to find, all you do is look for the cars parked outside and the satellite dish on the roof of his house."

"What is his address?"

"This I do not know; all I know is that the house is really big and that there are statues out front, with palm trees," Hector said.

"Is that all you know, Hector?" Miguel asked.

"Yes, that is all I know for certain," replied Hector, thinking he might live through the night. Finally, looking up at the gringos, Hector continued speaking. "Please, this is all I know."

Miguel, looking at Lucas, said, "Should we let him live or should we put him out of his misery?"

"Let him live, this way he will have a tale to tell his grandkids. Besides, he won't be able to do anything else, except talk to them."

By now Hector started thanking the two gringos for not killing him. At this point, realizing he was slowly dying, he looked up, saying to them both, "Stupid Americans, you think you are all so smart. You look for the men who took your President, thinking you can get him back. Maybe he might not want to come back. What would you think of that?"

Hector, seeing that the two gringos were speechless by his question, started to laugh at them, to which Miguel said, "The difference is these two gringos are walking out of here right now and you're not."

Hector wasn't laughing anymore with Miguel's reply, and as Miguel and Lucas left the building, Hector was screaming out to them, "You can't leave me like this."

Lucas, looked at Miguel, "Give me a second and I'll be right back."

Lucas went back into the building and, finding Hector where they had left him, walked up to him, "You know, Hector, you are right. We won't leave you like this."

Hector stopped crying and started smiling at Lucas, "Oh thank you, senor, I knew you wouldn't leave me here to die."

"You want to bet?" said Lucas, shooting Hector through the head and walking away.

After Lucas caught up with Miguel they headed back over the border, calling Bertrand. "We found the men that brought the terrorists across the border and we found out the boss is in Mexico City. We are headed that way now. All we know is that he lives close to the airport in a big fancy house with a satellite dish on top of the roof."

"Let me do some checking for you and see if I can help find the house for you," Bertrand replied.

"Let us know what you find; otherwise, we have some old contacts down there that we can call upon," Miguel said.

Once they boarded the flight from Nogales to Mexico City, they sat in their seats and slept all the way. Arriving in Mexico City several hours later, they departed the plane and were met at the gate by Police Chief Ruiz, who was decked out in his uniform. When Lucas and Miguel saw him standing there, they pretended to be amazed at his uniform and medals, asking for his autograph. Finally, Ruiz had to stop them from carrying on, "Welcome to Mexico City once again. Bertrand called me about what had happened to the President and the terrorists taking him here to our city."

"Can you help us with this?" Miguel asked.

"I think I may be able to. I have looked over the areas around the airport where this house is supposed to be, and I think I have found it."

Walking out of the terminal and getting into Ruiz's car, they left the airport to see if they could find the right house. Talking as they drove to the house, Miguel asked, "How are things in the police department now?"

"Very much better," said Ruiz as he continued, "The police department is basically clean, and all of the old police officers have been replaced with new people. The old police chief has been sent to prison for a very long time, along with the assistant to the governor and the mayor."

"Sounds like a clean sweep for the whole town, then," Lucas said.

"Yes, it has been as you say, a clean sweep," Ruiz said.

After another five minutes of driving Ruiz pulled up in front of the house thought to be the cartel boss's home.

"What do you know of this cartel boss?" Miguel asked.

"First of all, I know he is very well connected with the higher-ups in the political scene and is considered to be a friend to the President of Mexico and has connections outside our country to other people in high places there as well."

"What's his name?"

"His name is Diego Alvarez. From what I know of him he is clean. And if he is involved with the drug trade, he has other people do his work for him so that his hands stay clean. I have looked into his background and have not found anything questionable on him. He has made his money in electronics and computer software."

"Is there anyone else who lives around here that may be involved with the drug trade?" Lucas asked.

"Yes, there is one more place that may be of interest to you."

Driving to the other side of the airport, the police chief took them to another suburb, where the houses were well established. You could tell by looking at the homes and the cars parked in the driveways that the neighborhood was quite affluent. The cars were either BMWs, Mercedes, or Cadillacs. Driving through the neighborhood, you could tell the standard of living was high. The manicured lawns were picture perfect with metal fences around most of the housing properties. As they drove, they stopped at one house that was more palatial than the others on the street.

"This house belongs to Alfred Montoya. He is a bank President over one of the largest banks in Mexico City. He is well known for his charitable work among the poor of Mexico City," Ruiz said.

Miguel nudged Lucas and pointed at the roof of the house, both of them looked at the roof and saw a big dish antenna mounted on it. "What more do you know of this man, Montoya?" Lucas asked.

"Nothing more, except he travels a lot throughout South America and Mexico. As you can see, he has his own security for himself and family," Ruiz said, pointing out the man standing there with a radio in one hand and a holstered gun on his thigh.

"Would you like to meet Montoya? I know him from where I work now. We provide security for some of the parties he has given for charity work."

"Not at this time, possibly later, though," Miguel said.

"Well then, these are the only two that I know of that have satellite dishes on their homes. I will return you to the airport so that you can rent a car to drive around Mexico City. If you need anything from me, please let me know and I will do what I can."

"Thank you very much for your time and effort in helping us in this," Lucas said.

As they drove back to the airport to pick up a rental car, all was quiet and uneventful. Dropping them off, each said their goodbyes and Ruiz drove off, leaving them standing in front of the car-rental place. Miguel and Lucas walked in and picked up a car for their stay in Mexico City. Throwing their overnight bags into the trunk of the car, they drove over to the consulate to talk to the U.S. Ambassador to Mexico. Finding a place to park, they walked into the U.S. Embassy, passing the marine guard who stood there as security and going in to talk to the duty officer of the day.

Showing their badges to the duty officer, Miguel announced, "We are involved in the investigation of the President's kidnapping and we would like to talk to the U.S. Ambassador for a moment to see if anything new has occurred since we left Nogales."

The duty officer called the ambassador's secretary to see if she had time to visit with Miguel and Lucas about the kidnapping of the President. After hanging up, the duty officer looked at Miguel and Lucas. "She will let us know shortly."

A few moments later the secretary called back to the duty officer saying that the ambassador had just a few minutes in between meetings to visit. Lucas and Miguel were escorted to the office of the ambassador, who after recognizing them as they entered, said, "So what brings you two lugs back to Mexico City?"

"We're looking for the terrorists who kidnapped the President. Our information tells us they passed through here and we're here to find them, if possible," Miguel said.

"What can you tell us about the goings-on lately in Mexico City?" Lucas asked.

"Well, to tell you the truth, we haven't heard anything about the terrorists' activities here in Mexico City. In fact, it has been really quiet, considering all that's happened with the President being kidnapped," the ambassador said as she offered them a seat.

"What can you tell us about this Alfred Montoya?" Miguel asked. "From my understanding he is a very wealthy banker here in the city."

Looking at the duty officer, she motioned for him to leave. As he did so, he closed the door behind him. The ambassador looked at Miguel and Lucas. "He's dirty, based upon our Intel. How dirty he is we don't know yet. We ran a check on his financials from his bank not too long ago and found some interesting things going on. Seems that his bank is involved with some kind of money laundering for some questionable businesses here in Mexico City. Mind you, we were asked to look into it for the specific reason of finding where the money trail started."

"What did you find out by following the money trail?" Miguel asked.

"Well, we found that he is the intermediary for a lot of the drug cartels all through Mexico and South America. He is the major player in the game of drugs and other businesses that aren't even part of the drug scene."

"Do you think he is a cartel captain in the drug business?" Miguel asked.

"We haven't been able to prove that, although I wouldn't be surprised if he was."

"Do you know if he has contacts in America that he uses for his business ventures?"

"It would only seem reasonable to have them with his connections in the banking system. I would check with your contacts with the FBI and or maybe DEA to find that out."

"We'll do that. Is there anything else you can tell us about some of his friends and coworkers?" Lucas asked.

"There is a guy that works for him that's got an electronics business that is used for laundering money as well. I think if you find him he might lead you to the others involved."

"Do you think they could be involved with terrorists and kidnapping the President?" Lucas asked.

"That I can't say for sure; however, that being said, I'm sure these two would know the right people, who would be involved with them."

"Thank you for your time. You have been most helpful once again."

"Don't be strangers; come back anytime you need assistance on anything."

The two of them shook hands with the ambassador and left the office with the duty officer leading the way out of the building. When Miguel and Lucas got back into their car, they sat there for a minute trying to digest all that had been said to them about the banker and the electronics business owner. Lucas looked at Miguel. "Who do we go after first in this?"

"Just like the ambassador said, the little man first, then the banker. I wonder if we are going to run out of time before we find the President?" Miguel asked.

"Yeah, I wonder about that, too. Maybe we need to call Bertrand and let him know what we have found out down here."

"I think we should wait until we have better information about these two men before we contact Bertrand."

"As you wish. I know making a decision based on no information isn't the best way to proceed."

"Well then, let's get started following the electronics guy. Who knows, he may lead us to the banker and some of his friends."

The long process of staking out the electronics dealer began, and having no one else to check on, they stayed with him throughout the day. For a period of two days they followed the dealer to and from his house and job. Seeing nothing out of the ordinary, Miguel and Lucas started thinking that they needed a new plan to act on. Toward the end of the second day, staked out in front of his office out of sight, a car drove up that was being chauffeured, and as the driver got out of the car to open the door, Miguel nudged Lucas, who was reading a book, to look up. As they both watched the man get out of the car, Miguel started taking pictures of the guy. As he walked up to the office building, he was met by the dealer at the front door. Watching all this, Miguel looked over at Lucas. "Bingo!"

Lucas got out of the car and walked over to the building, dressed in the clothing of a safety inspector. He entered the building and followed the two men inside. As the two men continued walking, Lucas stopped at the front desk. The receptionist, looking up from her computer, "May I help you?"

"Hello, my name is Lucas. I'm here to do a spot safety inspection of the building to see if it is up to code."

The receptionist, looking at her appointment book, said, "I see you are not listed for having an appointment in our book."

"Yes, ma'am, you are right, it is supposed to be a spot inspection sort of, no notice type of inspection."

The receptionist looked at Lucas, "I don't think I can let you in to inspect without permission from my boss."

"I'm sorry to hear that. This has been scheduled for the last two weeks, and If I don't get it done today, I could lose my job. Besides, it will only take a minute or two and then I'll be gone."

By now Lucas was smiling sweetly at the receptionist, and the pleading look in his eyes finally worked on the lady. "Oh, all right, go ahead, but make it quick. I don't want to lose my job because of you either."

With that, Lucas went through the building, going through the closets where the chemicals were stored and each office, checking the smoke alarms and fire extinguishers where they were listed as being. Once outside the company President's office, he found a maintenance closet close by and went into the closet to see if he could hear the conversation between the two men inside the office. From what he could tell, the two men were in a heated exchange that would be loud and then go back to their normal voices. Lucas got the gist of the conversation, that it was dealing with some bad news about some of the banker's people getting killed in Nogales. The banker was saying, "I knew we shouldn't have been involved with the terrorists' plan to kidnap the President."

"What's the matter, you got paid really well for the work done there," the company owner said.

"Yes, you are right. I just didn't think I would lose some of my best men in the process."

"That is sad about your men, but there are others that can fill their places and, who knows, they may actually be honest."

By now the receptionist was looking for Lucas, who was still in the closet listening to the conversation. When she opened the closet door, Lucas was busy writing down all of his findings for the closet. Once complete on the discrepancies, he handed the list to the secretary, "This is not good, look at this," pointing to the rags. "You have rags not properly taken care of next to the chemicals. And look at your closet; it is completely loaded with too many chemical containers that need to be put away properly and should be in a locked cabinet. Your safety manager should be fired over his lack of competence."

After explaining the writeups as they walked back to the receptionist desk, he left and headed back down to the front of the building. "I'll be back next week and all of these writeups had better be taken care of. Otherwise, your company will have to be fined for this."

The receptionist looked at the list of writeups. "I'll get our safety man up here right now and have him take care of this."

"You better; otherwise, it's going to be his job on the line."

As he left the building, he walked over to the car and, sliding in on the passenger side of the car, he said, "Miguel, they are in it deep, real deep."

After explaining to Miguel what he heard inside the office from the two men, Lucas said, "I think we need to follow the banker. He seems to have lost the most and is probably the one who can't lose anymore."

Miguel, thinking for a minute, agreed with Lucas, "What do we do now so that he'll tip his hand so that we can nail him for the terrorist connection?"

"Let's play it by ear and see what shakes out."

"Okay, we'll play it out to see what happens."

They decided to follow the banker and see where it led. Starting their car, they waited for the banker to come out and get back into his car, so they could follow him. They were about two car lengths behind the limousine as they followed him back to the bank. In the meantime, Miguel contacted Bertrand. "We have information on a banker named Alfred Montoya being involved with the terrorists that kidnapped the President. What more can you get on him for us? Also, would you check out another man by the name of Diego Alvarez. He owns an electronics business and he is thought to be conspiring with the banker and the terrorists as well."

Bertrand quickly wrote the two names down. "We'll look into the financials and see where it leads us."

"We are following the banker right now and we're hoping it will lead us to a contact in the terrorist group," Miguel said.

"Proceed with caution; we can't afford to lose you guys down there. In the meantime, I'll let you know what we have found as soon as I have something on these two people."

"Not to worry, we don't want to get hurt or killed down here either. Please let us know what you find when you get the information. Oh, one other thing, would you check to see if the banker has any connections in Europe or the Middle East and also along the coastal towns in Mexico."

"Will do and again we'll let you know as quickly as we can once we get the information."

Miguel, ending his call, looked at Lucas, who was driving the car, "We need to find out his connections in the shipping business and in other countries."

"How do we do that?"

"I don't know yet. I'm still trying to figure that out myself. At least, we know who was involved with the terrorists down here. Let's just sit tight until we get word back from Bertrand."

Over the next couple of days Miguel and Lucas followed both the banker and the dealer, trying to find their connection with the kidnapping of the President and the group responsible for it. While waiting on Bertrand to get them the information on both of them, Lucas and Miguel found out through Ruiz that both men were involved with laundering cartel money by sending money through the local and offshore banks in the Cayman Islands on different projects being overseen by the bank in Mexico City.

When Bertrand did call them back with what he had found, it was a great big puzzle that needed someone to put together the completed picture of the puzzle. Bertrand said, "First off, this banker knows what he's doing with his money, as well as the others that deposit their money into the bank. It was hard to find the money trails because of all the dummy corporations set up for the laundering."

"What did you find out?" asked Lucas.

"Well, it isn't just his money, but it looks as if the money being routed through the bank is actually money from different leaders from all over the world. This money is being brought in by transfers to the main banks in the islands, then sent back out to the regular banks, who in turn use the money to set up businesses all over the world for the depositors to funnel more money back to their savings accounts."

"Is there any connection between the banker and the terrorists?"

"Yes, I'd say about ten to twenty connections with the bank's money and other people's money as well. It seems that this bank is paying the terrorists money in supporting their cause by allowing them to buy weapons from all over the world."

"How's that possible when the terrorists are considered poor?"

"Somebody higher up is paying this terrorist group money to purchase their weapons and transportation between our country and the Middle East in order to accomplish their desires. If I didn't know any better, I'd think they are using ISIS and Saudi Arabia's monetary network as a way to keep themselves afloat financially."

"How do you want to handle this from here?" Miguel asked.

"We really don't know what to do at this point, except keep following the money trail in the banking system."

"Can we break into the computer system and siphon the money out of several accounts and put the money into the banker's account and show the depositors that he's taking money out of their accounts and stealing it for his own account?"

"There's an idea. Let me look into it. Maybe we can freeze the account if we can find proof that the money is being laundered for the cartel," Bertrand said.

"I think I have an idea that might help you with catching and finding the cartel's money."

"What do you have in mind?"

"I don't really know yet, but if it works you'll know it when you see it."

"Until we hear from you or see things happening from down there, we'll keep checking the bank's business and financial records and try to sort this out from our end. Maybe we can shut him down from here."

"We'll let you go, and if anything turns up let us know and vice versa as well. Goodbye."

Miguel, looking at the confused look on Lucas's face, "We need to get with Ruiz and see if he can assist us in this game of deception."

"You lead the way and I'll follow."

Driving over to the police station, Miguel and Lucas asked the police chief's secretary if they could speak to the police chief. Getting up from her desk and walking into the chief's office, she came back a few seconds later and showed them the way to his office. Ruiz was surprised to see them and gestured for them both to sit down. With Miguel and Lucas sitting comfortably, Ruiz asked, "What can I do for you today?"

"We would like to tell you that our sources say that the banker and the electronics dealer are in bed with the terrorists who kidnapped our President a couple days ago," Miguel said.

The Chief looked at Miguel, "Are you sure about this?"

"We have proof, but the problem is that it's tied up in the banking system via financial documents. Lucas was able to overhear a conversation between the banker and the electronics dealer at his office, verifying that the banker used his own people to get the terrorists in and out of America and, most likely, back to the Middle East by now."

"What do you need from me at this point?"

"We need to break into the bank and steal some of the money, and we need your help."

Chapter V

The shocked look on Ruiz's face was indescribable, and Lucas was just as surprised by what Miguel had said. With the looks of disbelief, Miguel started to laugh. Ruiz and Lucas weren't sure what to do at this point of the conversation.

"Pardon me, could you say that one more time?" Ruiz asked.

"I'm kidding about stealing the money; what I want to do is shift the funds around to make it look like someone stole the money," Miguel said.

"How do you plan to do that?" asked Lucas, finally speaking after the shock of hearing what Miguel said wore off.

"I'm not quite sure yet. Let me explain what I mean."

With that, Miguel went on to explain the idea he had and what needed to be done in order to make it happen. Afterwards Ruiz and Lucas sat there for a moment, thinking to themselves. "You know, that Might work," said Ruiz.

"Do you have anybody that works at the bank that you can trust, who will work with us on this?" Miguel asked.

Ruiz sat back a moment, thinking, then said, "I Might know of one person who would be willing to help us in this plan of yours."

Picking up the phone, he called his secretary into his office, "Will you get me Mr. Sanchez on the phone; you should have his number at the bank handy."

The secretary left the office and within minutes had Mr. Sanchez on the phone, waiting to talk to Ruiz. "Can you meet me for lunch today? I have something to talk to you about." Ruiz asked Mr. Sanchez.

After a moment or two the lunch date was set, and all was in order for the meet. Within the hour all three of them met with Mr. Sanchez in the local café to discuss Miguel's plan with him. After ordering their food and getting their drinks, Miguel went on to explain his idea to Mr. Sanchez about moving money around into different accounts. At first, Mr. Sanchez just sat and listened to Miguel's idea and then, looking at each of them, said, "Why would I want to do this for you?"

"I understand your feelings about this. The reason we want your assistance in this is because your boss was involved with the kidnapping of our President and bringing down Air Force One, killing a lot of innocent people."

"And?"

"And we know he is the one they used to get the terrorists to and from America in order to do it."

"And?"

By now Miguel was getting perplexed by Mr. Sanchez's questions and lack of concern. "And we believe he is involved in moving drugs from your country to our country."

This statement from Miguel seemed to strike Mr. Sanchez the hardest. You could see it in his eyes more so than anywhere else. "Please continue," Mr. Sanchez said.

"We believe that your boss and another man who runs an electronics company. . ."

At this point Mr. Sanchez spoke up. "You don't mean Diego Alvarez, do you?"

"Yes, as a matter of fact, we do mean Mr. Alvarez."

"What do want me to do?" Mr. Sanchez asked.

"Why, all of a sudden, do you want to help us in this?" Lucas asked.

"Mr. Alvarez is a known money handler for the cartel and has been for quite a while. I have brought this information up numerous times to the bank president, to no avail. It seems that the president was well aware of this fact and chose to do nothing about it, which told me he was involved with it somehow as well. Please believe me when I say that the bank is a good place for most of our customers but I feel that it has become a cesspool of drug money being moved from one place to another. I would only do this for the integrity of the bank and to get rid of the smell of dirty money."

"We would like you to move some money into the account of Diego from an outside source. This source should be from a known drug dealer. And then bring it to Montoya's attention. Then take the money from Alvarez's account and put it into Montoya's account, and let Alvarez know about it, just enough to create suspicion on both their parts towards each other. Then just sit back and watch the fireworks begin."

Mr. Sanchez sat back and thought about what the plan was and smiled for a second about it. "This should be easy to do. When do you want me to do this?"

"Soon, if not sooner," Miguel said. He continued, "It has to look as if Diego is running his own drug operation and Montoya has gotten greedy once he found out about it. Can you do it?"

"Yes, I can. My only concern is how do we make sure it stays aboveboard for the bank and myself?"

"That's the reason we have the police chief here to vouch for us. But to show we are being honest ourselves, Ruiz here will also be involved with the investigation of the two people we're after, also to make sure that he's in the loop and has your permission to be part of it. In the end, he will provide top cover for you as we start this adventure, so you will be safe."

At this point Ruiz said, "I can personally speak for these two guys, they both are federal agents with the FBI and I have worked with them in getting one of the cartel guys off the street, plus a few other political players."

Mr. Sanchez, looking at the police chief and thinking out loud, said, "Are these the two men that helped get rid of our crooked police chief and the mayor's number-one man?"

Ruiz nodded his head yes, adding, ". . .and also helped me get rid of all the bad cops on the force."

"Okay, that's good enough for me to want to work with you guys."

"The police chief will be the monitor and liaison between you and us for all of the actions you take in the bank and will be waiting for your inputs. From there we will do the rest to get Alvarez caught with the drugs and the money. I want it understood we aren't about stealing any money. It must appear as if the money disappeared and then was put back. What we want to make sure of is that no money will ever leave the bank. All of the money transactions will be on your end, Mr. Sanchez, and we will take care of the rest ourselves. You will be the one that will be moving things around," Miguel said.

Mr. Sanchez nodded his head, saying, "I understand completely, I wouldn't be involved if the money did leave the bank. Where should we meet for the next meeting?"

"Right here seems to be fine for us; how about you two?" Miguel said.

"This place is good as any," Mr. Sanchez replied.

"Works for me as well," Ruiz said.

"Then it's agreed," Lucas stated.

After the meeting was concluded Mr. Sanchez walked out with Ruiz, asking, "Can we trust these two men?"

"With my life," Ruiz said. "They have done more for Mexico City than you can imagine."

Mr. Sanchez was surprised by the reply and kept walking to his car. After getting in he drove back to the bank and walked into his office and sat down at his desk. Using his password, he unlocked his computer and started to figure out what to do next for his part of the plan. Typing in Diego Alvarez's name and looking at the history of withdrawals and transactions for him, he found a discrepancy that would work in favor of the plan. Seeing a minor glitch in the amount of money being deposited into his account, he added a couple of thousand dollars by transferring money from Montoya's account into Alvarez's account. Mr. Sanchez thought to himself, *"This should be seen by the bank president tomorrow morning."* He called Ruiz to let him know what he had done. He then went back to work as usual and started making sure all of the other loan applications were in order.

Miguel waited for the police chief to come back after speaking with Mr. Sanchez. Once he returned, Miguel asked Ruiz to borrow some of his confiscated drugs from lockup and place them at Alvarez's home, as if it were a delivery to him. He then made sure to have pictures taken of the drug drop-off at the house. He then asked Ruiz to start investigating Alvarez for buying drugs with the intent to sell by going to the president of the bank to ask questions about Alvarez's business actions.

Ruiz went into the contraband lockup room and signed out three kilos of heroin, which had been confiscated from another case. Taking the drugs and placing them in a plastic bag, he then drove to Alvarez's house. Picking the lock on the front door, he walked in and placed the drugs in the bedroom closet, then took pictures of the drugs lying on the floor. After he took the pictures he brought the drugs back to the police building and signed them back into lockup for safekeeping. Ruiz went back to his daily business of running the department. Being notified by Ruiz that the investigation was beginning, Miguel and Lucas waited outside Alvarez's place to see what would happen next.

The next day, when bank president Montoya arrived at his office and started checking his e-mail messages from the night before, there was a notification of action done in his personal bank account. Opening the e-mail and seeing that money from his personal account had been deposited into Alvarez's account, he was surprised to see that two thousand dollars had been deposited there. Thinking this was unusual, he checked to see if the two thousand dollars actually went into the account. Opening up Alvarez's account, he saw that the money had been placed into the account the day before. Quickly removing the amount from Alvarez's bank account, he thought of it as being a computer error by the bank. Having accomplished this, he continued going through the rest of his e-mails. Then after checking his calendar with his secretary, he started his day at the bank.

The police chief, looking at his watch, decided that it was time to start the second step of the investigation by going to visit Montoya at his office. After lunch he went to the bank and said to Montoya's secretary, "I would like to visit with the president about an issue that requires his attention."

"May I tell him the nature of your visit?" she said as she stood up to notify the president.

"No, it's of a personal nature."

Montoya came out of his office to greet the police chief and, after shaking hands with him, they both walked back into his office, closing the door behind them. Ruiz proceeded to show the pictures of the drugs found at Alvarez's house. "Do you have any idea if Mr. Alvarez is involved with buying and selling drugs?" Ruiz asked.

"None that I'm aware of," he replied.

"Is there a chance we can look at his financial records just to see if there has been any money transferred into his account recently?"

"It shouldn't be a problem at all to review his bank records."

After bringing up the records for Mr. Alvarez, Montoya noticed that another five thousand dollars had been put into his account earlier that day. Showing Ruiz the financial records of Alvarez, Ruiz could see for himself the money had been recently deposited into Alvarez's account. Montoya thought this was unusual for Alvarez to be having money deposited into his account twice in less than a week. Montoya showed the computer screen depicting Alvarez's account to the police chief, who studied it for a moment and then said, "It looks as if a couple of transactions have taken place recently."

"Yes, it does show transactions for today and last Monday morning, as well," the banker said.

"Can you tell me where the transactions originated from?"

"Not by looking at this screen; it will take one of my computer people to track down where the money came from. This may take a couple of days to figure it out."

After hearing this, Ruiz asked, "When would be a good time to find out what's going on?"

"Call me on Friday and we'll go from there."

After getting up from his chair, Ruiz shook the bank president's hand, "Until then," he said as he walked out of his office.

The banker sat back down in his chair deep in thought, he was also very interested in finding out who was responsible for these money transactions himself. With the police chief being involved, especially, with the pictures of the drugs being found at Alvarez's house, he began to wonder what was going on with Alvarez. Had he gotten greedy or was there some other reason for the drugs being there? Just like the police chief, he needed answers. This wasn't the first time that Alvarez wanted to work on his own in the drug trade; in fact, that's how the banker first heard of him being involved with the drug scene in Mexico City. The only reason Alvarez wasn't already in jail for selling drugs was because of his good timing when the cartel approached the banker with the offer of more money in his pocket through laundering their drug money for them. Alvarez's business was the ideal place to wash the money, with the bank offering loans that would entail using the cartel's drug money to start up his electronics business.

Alvarez had gotten smarter over the years since he had started working with the banker. Perhaps he was thinking of leaving the banker and striking out on his own again, expanding his electronics business by building more stores in other areas of the city using the laundered money to invest in his company. The banker thought about this for a moment and shook his head *no* to the idea. No matter what, the bank was the only way for the drug money to be laundered on the scale the cartel needed to do it. So, what was the game Alvarez was playing now? Was there another player that was trying to get into the game, as well? The banker had to know for his own sake and had to know sooner than later. The question now was how to approach Mr. Alvarez without letting him know he was onto his game. Could it be that Alverez was the one who had the banker's people killed up north along the border? Again, more questions than answers.

Chapter VI

Bertrand picked up the phone and called Sam Hatfield. Sam answered the phone, "FBI Special Agent Sam Hatfield speaking."

"Sam, this is Bertrand calling to let you know that we've found a connection with the terrorists and two key players in Mexico City. A bank president and an electronics businessman, both are involved with money laundering and the drug business in Mexico City. The terrorists used the connections of the bank president to get in and out of the country with our President. Lucas and Miguel are working to find out more information on the two of them. But, for sure, they were involved with the terrorists getting into America via Mexico."

"That's good news. What are their names?" Sam asked.

"The banker's name is Alfred Montoya. He's the president of the biggest bank in Mexico City. The electronics dealer is Diego Alvarez. Both of them were heard in a conversation together, talking about the loss of some of their people in Nogales. That's when the terrorists' connection came up in the conversation."

Quickly writing their names down on a pad of paper, Sam asked, "What do you have on them, anything worthwhile?"

"Nothing concrete as yet. That's what Miguel and Lucas are trying to find out now."

"How soon do you think you'll know more?"

"Hard to say, Sam, they're trying some sort of game to ferret out their connections to the terrorists. One thing for sure, though, is the banker travels a lot overseas to do business for his bank. I was thinking you might try that angle to see what you can find from your side."

"Let me do some checking and if anything turns up, I'll let you know as soon as I can."

"Fair enough. Will talk to you later, then. Goodbye."

"Goodbye, and tell your two guys, good work!"

As Sam hung up the phone, he sat and thought for a moment about what Bertrand had told him. Finally, a break in the case. Looking at his watch, it was now 3:00 p.m. Checking his computer, he decided to run the names of the banker and the electronics dealer to see what would come up in the system. After a couple of minutes, the names came up blank for anything of use. From all outward appearances, they were clean, law-abiding citizens of their country.

Sam called his team of agents and, looking at them, realized for the first time they were all brand-new FBI agents, all probably working their first case ever under his tutelage. As they gathered together in his office, he said, "Well, kids, we got our first break in the case from our friends down in Mexico City. It seems as if a bank president and an electronics businessman are involved with the terrorists that kidnapped the President. What I need from you kids is whatever information you can find on these two people. Jennifer, I want you and your team to take the lead on finding out about Alfred Montoya. Bill, I want you and your team to take the lead on finding out about Diego Alvarez. I want to know when they get up in the morning, what they have for breakfast, and what the two of them are wearing to work. You'll need to find out who they talk to and when and where they do it. Do you kids understand? And I want to know about it yesterday."

Bill and Jennifer nodded their heads in agreement, and with their team of agents they headed out to their desks; and as each team gathered around Bill and Jennifer, they received their marching orders as to what their responsibilities would be. For the next three hours, all the agents were busy searching and looking for anything that would help find the President and bring him home.

As Sam watched his "kids" working, he was impressed with their desire to do what was necessary. Bill Williams and Jennifer Smith were in the top of their graduating class in the academy at Quantico two years ago and, hence, why Sam put them in as team leads. The other members of the team were brand new, right out of the Academy. The hardest part for Sam was that they were about ten to fifteen years younger than he was. He had always felt like, *I'm not getting older, the kids are just getting younger*. He, of course, knew the truth but he would never admit it to himself, for fear that he *was* getting older in real life. But for now, he was the "old Man" and they were the new kids on the block. Sam and the team worked through the night, looking for anything that would give them a clue about these two men from Mexico, but by 1:00 am nothing had been uncovered yet. Finally, telling the kids to go home for the night, Sam said he would see them in the morning bright and shiny to pick up where they left off. Watching the last of them leave, he left, as well, to his hotel room to get some much needed sleep.

The next morning Sam showed up, as usual, at the normal time and, opening the door, he found both teams already in place working. He was amazed but didn't show it to the kids. He just went into his office and sat down for a minute before coming out to get himself some coffee. Looking at the two teams working, he wondered when they had come in to start work. Checking his e-mail first thing, he found nothing of interest to reply to, that couldn't wait till later. At this point he called in Bill and Jennifer, "Well, what have you two found since yesterday?"

Bill looked at Jennifer. "Ladies first."

"What we have found on the banker, so far, is that he does a lot of traveling over to the Middle East and has business connections in Syria, Iran, Iraq, and Somalia, and parts of Germany."

"What kind of business are we talking about?" Sam asked.

"Well, that's hard to say at this point, simply because we see no business coming out of any of his contacts overseas."

"What does that mean?"

"Well, sir, what we see is a lot of travel but with nothing coming from it. No products, no new businesses being created. All we see are his business dealings with companies that don't exist anymore."

"What are we going to do about that, Jennifer?"

Jennifer stood there for a moment before answering the question. "Well, I have my team calling the CIA and the State Department, checking their contacts for further Intel on the businesses over in Germany and the Middle East to see what they have for us to work with."

Sam sat there for a second and looked at Bill. "Well, what do you have for me, Bill?"

"We found out that Mr. Alvarez travels with the banker on some of his trips, peddling his electronics all over the Middle East. So far, most of his business connections are in Germany and France. But we also have found some of his electronic stuff in Syria and Somalia."

"What kind of stuff are we talking about?"

"Electronic eavesdropping equipment and satellite electronics from Germany for which he acts as a liaison for the Middle Eastern companies."

"Have you found any information on the companies yet?"

"Not yet, we are reaching out just like Jennifer's team to find out about the companies via the CIA and State department."

"What are you going to do about it if you can't get the information you need?"

Bill stood there for a minute, not sure what to say at first. "We could send some people over there to do a look-around."

"Who do you suggest we send over there to do that?"

By now Bill was stuck for answers and shook his head. "I don't know who we can send over there."

"Were you planning on telling me of your dilemma, or were you going to let me figure it out myself?"

Bill turned slightly red in the face and said nothing, just standing there looking at the floor of Sam's office. Sam had given Bill a hard time, not for show but for teaching. Jennifer was standing there watching all of this, as well, knowing she could be next in Sam's sites.

At this point Sam said, "Kids, you need to know that when you hit the wall at whatever you're doing, don't be afraid to ask for assistance in getting your job done. The goal here is to realize your limits and know where to go to get past them. It's understood that you will not be able to do everything yourself. But at the same time, don't sell yourselves short thinking you're being lazy. Do you understand what I'm saying to you?"

Both of them nodded their heads and said, "Yes." With some of the heat taken off them, Sam looked at them. "Let me look into this. I have some connections that may be of use to us in this situation. Oh, by the way, good work. Now get your butts out of here and go get me some more intel."

Both Jennifer and Bill were smiling again as they went out of Sam's office, ready to continue their assigned tasks. Sam smiled to himself as the two of them left his office, thinking, *"These kids are good, in fact, really good."*

Sam picked up his phone and called his superiors to let them know of the progress of his team in the investigation. Once he cleared his portion of the brief, he asked to see what kind of support they could get overseas to check out these companies that were doing business with the banker from Mexico. The supervisors were needing time to check into his requests to go further outside the country for verification of these supposed companies in the Middle East and Europe. Leaving the conference with a tentative "We'll get back to you on this," the meeting was over. Sam closed out the conference with one thought, *"We know they have support from ISIS, but someone else is running this kidnapping, and we need to find out who it is."*

After the meeting it was time for another cup of coffee and to go see what was happening with the teams again. This time Sam just walked around and watched the kids do their thing in trying to find out more answers for their part of the investigation. Not saying anything, he sat there listening to the kids make phone calls all over the world via the State Department and CIA analysts who, in their own way, were also doing their own investigations looking for the President. The CIA had the wherewithal to do the on-ground checks needed to find out about companies in the Middle East and Europe and, of course, they would want credit for helping the FBI in their investigation. The FBI didn't care about credit, simply because the President's life was on the line. The credit given could be like a double-edged sword, not only could it be used as a pat on the back, it could also be used as a kick in the pants if they failed. The time for political infighting was at an end. The common goal would be, and should be, finding the

President, no matter what. Blast the politics, just get the job done.

With this new information, the CIA sent for two of their agents already in the field and had them start looking into the companies identified by the FBI for possible terrorist connections. The two men selected were Dan and John, who had previously worked together on a case in Iraq. Their expertise in getting the job done without all the fanfare was one of their trademarks that only the CIA could appreciate. Being called in to start checking the companies was considered high priority, and with both of them working together, hopefully, the light could be shed on this new terrorist organization.

John, who caught sight of Dan first, looked at him. "Where did they find you, in the middle of the desert? They must have dug pretty deep to get you."

Dan, recognizing the voice, looked around to see John standing there looking at him and exclaimed, "They must have had to dig deeper to find *you*, huh?"

Both of them hugged each other and, shaking hands, John asked, "Do you know what's going on here?"

"Not a clue, except something about going on vacation somewhere in the Middle East again."

Dan and John were picked up by helicopter and then transported by aircraft into the middle of the desert and flown to CIA field headquarters, Doha, located in Qatar, which was a part of the United Arab Emirates. They were briefed as to what their mission would be, which was they were to go into Somalia and find out what they could about a new terrorist organization called Al-Shebiib Jihadist Fundamentalist Group, supposedly involved with the kidnapping of the President. These terrorists were considered more dangerous than ISIS and Al-Qaeda combined. The threat of the two Americans being caught was high, and chances of surviving the mission was slim. That being said, the CIA had given Dan and John permission to protect themselves and, therefore, any action required of them would be considered appropriate in order to survive.

After the briefing, Dan and John looked at each other and wondered what they were getting themselves into. Dan looked at John and, as their eyes met, you could see the look of doubt in both their eyes about returning from this mission. Dan looked at John, dubiously, "Just another walk in the park, don't you think, Danny boy?"

"Yeah, right, more like a walk in the local mine field in the middle of the night, blindfolded."

Dan and John were given the material and supplies they would need for being in the deserts of Djibouti and Somalia. The plan was for them to land in east Djibouti, closest place next to Somalia, then hike into the town of Hargeisa, Somalia, and then start looking for the leader of the Al-Shebiib Jihadist Fundamentalist Group and, if possible, bleed him for intel, if not able, to terminate with prejudice. There was one point of contact they could rely on for help in Hargeisa, an old woman named Hagath, who would be in her late 60's. She was once married to a prince from Ethiopia and had moved over to Somalia because of the famine, after her husband had died. They would be able to find her working the local bazaar, selling vegetables from her garden. As they listened, they were given a picture of her from twenty years earlier. A very beautiful lady in her day, no telling what she would look like now, though.

With the briefing completed, they loaded their stuff onto their backs and walked out to the airplane. After shaking hands with their handler, they boarded the military C-130 aircraft and took off. The flight was about five hours and would be a High Altitude Low Opening (HALO) jump at night. Having studied the maps, Dan and John put the material away before nodding off to sleep. The flight engineer woke them up about ten minutes out from their jump point. Putting on their parachutes and oxygen masks, the tail end of the aircraft opened up. Looking out into the darkness, all they could see were the stars in the sky above them. The flight engineer was watching the red light and waiting for it to turn green from the cockpit in front of the airplane. In two minutes, the light went from red to green and both men jumped out of the aircraft into the night at twenty thousand feet up. Free falling at a speed of 160 miles per hour, they fell into the darkness for five minutes, watching the illuminated altimeters which they wore on their wrists. They pulled their drag chutes at 3000 feet, which slowed their descent to 120 miles per hour, just enough for the main chutes to work when needed. At 2000 feet they deployed their main chutes and drifted down to earth at a slow 15 miles per hour. This gave them a chance to get their bearings before touching down. Each had a light tied to his legs so that they wouldn't crash into each other while free falling and also as a marker for when they landed in the desert, leastwise till they could get together. Landing in the sand of the desert made for a softer impact and an easier way of getting rid of their parachutes and other gear not needed for their trek through the desert. Burying their equipment, they found each other within minutes, with John making the call on the satellite phone to their handler, "Dry feet."

"Roger dry feet and good luck," the handler said.

The handler now went back to his office to relay the message to his superiors and then went to bed.

Dan and John got their bearings from the maps they had and the GPS on their satphone to verify the direction they needed to go to find the old woman in Hargeisa. It would take a few days to get there and traveling at night was the easiest way across the desert, especially if they didn't want to be seen by any of the local people.

Chapter VII

Assad walked through the jail into the back of the building, heading toward the cell that the President of the United States was sitting in. After asking the guard to leave, he waited until the guard had closed the door behind him before talking to the President. Assad opened the cell door and walked in and sat down next to the President. The President then commented, "It has been days since your last visit, what's the latest news?"

"I'm sorry, my friend, but we have not heard of any news about you, except from the newspapers from your country."

"Well, you know what they say, no news is good news."

"How are they treating you in here? I hope it's not too bad, Mr. President."

"Please, do not call me "President." We have been friends for too, too long for that to stand in the way. My name is Aaden Zakaria, as you well know."

"Yes, it is, and I apologize; but for the sake of our facade I must not allow myself to use your real name, leastwise for the moment."

"Yes, I see your point and I suppose you are right. Very well, then, we will play this charade until we can do otherwise. I think it is best for all of us, although I would appreciate, if it's possible, to have you keep bringing me the good food."

"My friend, I would consider it a pleasure to have you at dinner tonight, so I can interrogate you myself. Let's say about 7:00 p.m. Will that work for you, my friend?"

"I'm at your disposal, as always. One last thing, do you think you could contact my wife to let her know that I'm okay and that everything is going as planned?"

"Of course, we will send a message through the prescribed channel, like before. I'm sure she will appreciate the message."

"Thank you for understanding."

"I must tell you, the codes you brought with you have been working very well. We have been able to decipher the plans that the Israelis are using for their space defense system and have replaced their codes with ours to blow up the missiles as they launch from their pedestals. When we attack them with our own Scuds, we will take them by surprise, hitting all their major bases and cities."

"That is good. Anything to help our friends and brothers in this war against the infidels. I'm happy that the codes were of use to you. I feel it was the least I could do to help fight our holy war against them."

"It is time for me to leave now. Remember, I will call for you at seven tonight."

"I'll be looking forward to it."

Assad left the jail cell and locked the door behind him, telling the guards, as he always did, "Do not let anything happen to him."

As promised, Assad sent a message to the first lady through the normal channels that had been set up to let her know that the President was safe and sound for the time being. After he had completed the transmission to the first lady he went into his house and checked to see how the dinner preparations were going. Satisfied that everything was on schedule, he sat down in the den and waited for 7:00 to come.

Chapter VIII

With the President being kidnapped and possibly dead, Vice President Vance now took over the duties of running the country and, of course, his job was to receive the current Intel briefs from all of the alphabets on a regular basis. After each session with the Intel community he would have to make a decision as to how to handle different scenarios as they popped up all over the world. His major focus was still on finding the President and who had taken him and why they wanted such a big target to take.

Acting President Vance came from Oklahoma and was a liberal conservative before becoming a Vice-Presidential nominee. He was chosen for being a moderate in the Congress and because the people of America liked his cavalier attitude toward the world as a whole. Vance always took the opportunity to meet and greet new leaders and old leaders alike. His charm when running for the vice presidency happened to be the turning point for the President winning the election over a year ago.

Underneath that cavalier charm was a very shrewd man who knew politics like the back of his hand. He was no fool and wouldn't suffer fools when he became a congressman. He was considered spot-on in his thinking of how things should be in the country. In his own way, he was respected on both sides of the aisle for being fair but firm. When finding out about the President being kidnapped, he cancelled his vacation and immediately left his home state and returned to the White House to take over the duties and responsibilities of being President. The difference for him was he never wanted to be President. He had liked where he was and what he was doing for his own state and was content to do just that and nothing more.

As the time grew longer in finding the President, the more he hated being in charge of the country, not because he couldn't do it, but because of having all of these damn meetings that he didn't like to attend.

Three days later, in one of his Intel briefings, he was given the news that the FBI had a few leads they were checking out about Mexico and a terrorist group based in Somalia. This got Vance's ears. Stopping the briefing, he asked the FBI director, "Would you please repeat what you just said?"

The FBI director repeated what he had said, "The investigation is still in its infancy, but there is solid proof that one of the cartels was involved in getting the terrorists in and out of Mexico."

"I'm sure your agency is still working on a solution to this problem?"

"Yes, Mr. President, we are in the process of getting our people over there with the help of the Department of Defense (DOD)."

Vance looked at his generals as they nodded their heads in unison. "Very well, keep me posted on anything that comes from this, will you, Director? Is there anything else I need to be aware of at this point, gentlemen?" Vance asked, looking around the room at his Intel chiefs, one of the men from the National Security Agency (NSA) raised his hand, and Vance acknowledged him, "Go ahead Dave, what do you have for me?"

"Mr. President, I'm not sure if this is important or not. Our agency has been picking up transmissions emanating from Somalia for quite some time now, not on a regular basis, but enough to get our attention. We have our people trying to break the code and find out where it's coming from and where it's going to."

As the acting President considered what Dave had said, he asked, "What do you think about these transmissions?"

"We know that the transmissions have been going on since the election, and there was a flurry of chatter just before the President went to Chicago."

"What are you saying, Dave?"

"I'm not sure what I'm saying, Mr. President, except that we keep getting these transmissions periodically and then they're gone."

"From Somalia, huh?"

"Yes, Mr. President."

"Do you think it has anything to do with the kidnapping of the President?"

"This is just my opinion sir, but I believe it does."

"Anything else, ladies and gentlemen?"

As he went around the table, they all nodded their heads that their portion of the brief was complete. At this point Vance said his goodbyes, and for everybody that was the cue to leave. As the directors of the Intel community left the room, Vance looked at Dave, "Stick around for a moment, will you, Dave?"

"Yes, Mr. President."

After everybody cleared the conference room the acting President had Dave sit down next to him. As Dave pulled up the chair, he waited for Vance to ask him some more questions about these new transmissions coming from Somalia. "Please repeat to me your thoughts about these new signals coming from East Africa," Vance said.

"Well, sir, it's like this, about once a week we would pick up these coded transmissions coming from East Africa. At first, we thought nothing of them until we were told about a new terrorist group coming from Somalia. Then we started paying more attention to them, at least a little closer than before. We noticed a flurry of radio transmissions coming from that area of the world just before the President's plane went down. Then it picked up again right after we assumed the President was kidnapped."

"What are you saying, Dave? This time tell me what you want to say, we're big kids here."

"Well, sir, we never had picked up these signals until the President won the election. I hope you understand that what I'm trying to say is that I think that the President may be involved with his own kidnapping."

Vance just about fell out of his chair upon hearing what Dave had said. "Are you sure you know what you're saying here, Dave?"

"Sir, to be honest with you, I'm not sure about any of this, so far. All I know is that these signal transmissions are not all that random."

"What have you done to check this theory out?"

"I've got our best linguists working on this right now. Please understand, sir, I'm not sure about this and I'm not wanting to call the President anything other than just being at the wrong place at the wrong time."

Vance thought about what David had said. "I need you to keep this under wraps until you have proof one way or the other about your thoughts. I also want you to make this priority number one on breaking that code."

"Are you saying you believe what I'm telling you, Mr. President?"

"Let's just say you have piqued my curiosity for the time being. Keep me informed about anything that comes up on this."

Dave walked out of the President's conference room, feeling a little better about his concerns dealing with the kidnapping of the President. Vance waited until David had left the room before calling his private investigator. As he waited for the phone to be picked up by the private investigator, he sat there wondering about his own feelings and suspicions about the President. Upon hearing the voice on the other end, he related his new piece of information to the private investigator. The private investigator paused for a moment to allow what the acting President had said to him to sink in before proceeding. "That would make sense to me if the President was involved with his own kidnapping. How do you want me to proceed from here?"

"Keep an eye on the first lady, maybe she can show us what's been going on in the White House since the election."

"Will do."

With that, the phone line went dead. Vance went back to his normal activities that had been planned for the day. After checking with his secretary, as she went through the itinerary for the President, he realized he was going to hate the day. For him, it was just more meetings with his constituents and special groups looking for time with the President. He thought to himself, *"Why can't we have a war or natural catastrophe to worry about, instead of meetings?"* He smiled as he thought again about a war or natural catastrophe and said to himself, *"It's a little bit over the top just to avoid a meeting, don't you think, Vance?"*

With that, the day started for Vance and all of the other guests that were waiting to meet the President. Little did he know that in a few days his idea of war would be on the table as they sat in a crisis meeting dealing with the outcome of the attack against Israel.

Chapter IX

Out in the Golan Heights, overlooking all of Israel, two scouts were seated, watching a buildup of Syrian tanks along the border which separated Israel and Syria. Their position was just past Lake Tiberias and farther east, closer to Salkhad. The scouts reported from their position the activity of the tank buildup that they were watching. After they had contacted headquarters regarding what they had seen, the Israeli Air Force launched an Eitan Unmanned Aerial Vehicle (UAV) to fly over the area to photograph and confirm the report of the tank formation that had been forming near the border.

The Israelis were always watching the borders of their country since they had become a nation in 1947, always expecting another invasion and waiting for it to happen. When the pictures started coming in to the headquarters of the Chief of Staff, the duty officer recognized the tanks as being Soviet-built T-90s. Russia, being one of Syria's allies, had supplied them with T-90 1992 model tanks and later updated T-90A tanks in 2015 to add to their Tiger forces, which were considered the Syrians' point of the spear for any ground-assault attacks against Israel. Seeing these tanks away from their normal bases, the duty officer called his boss to let him know what was out in the desert on the border. This time, two fully loaded F-16s with antitank missiles were launched to reconnoiter the area where the tanks were. Flying at treetop level, they buzzed the tanks as they flew into Syrian airspace. As they climbed for altitude, they saw the rest of the equipment partially concealed with netting. This time, asking the controllers on the ground to send the UAV further into the Syrian air space, the UAV photographed the partially concealed Scud missiles on each side of the dirt road leading to the Israeli border. This sent a panic through the Israeli headquarters and the Chiefs of Staff were being briefed as to what was being seen by the UAV in real time. This was the first time that the Scuds had been set up this close to the Israeli border; consequently, the military chiefs decided that they would send in a special-forces unit to take them out before they were able to be used against them. In the meantime, they would try the diplomatic channels, figuring that it would be easier to ask for forgiveness rather than asking for permission to enter Syria to destroy the missiles.

The shockwave of a possible new war with their neighbors loomed on the horizon. Israel called upon the United Nations to convene a special meeting to deal with this new threat to Israel. The U.N. was slow in their response since no act of war had occurred and asked Syria what their intentions were with the tank buildup so close to Israel. Their reply was that it was a training exercise for their troops and equipment. Israel knew better than that. The question for Israel was whether to attack the Syrian Army first, thereby provoking a war, or stand by waiting for the Syrians to attack them. Israel now put their forces on full alert and started their war machine in the direction of Lake Tiberius. The Israeli Air Force was now on a one-minute alert status, with their UAVs flying over the border, watching the activity of the Syrian military, constantly reporting and photographing any activity that would show any attempt to launch a strike against Israel.

Because of the complaint filed with the U.N., America was notified as well, as it was part of the big three superpowers in the U.N. Acting President Vance was made aware of the situation and watched as it started to unfold, not being able to do anything. At this point he ordered the Joint Chiefs of Staff (JCS) to have their military resources start gathering imagery and intelligence in order to keep him in the loop if he had to act in Israel's behalf.

Once again, the Middle East was becoming a pain in the ass and a chess game for the rest of the world's greatest powers. Russia and China were watching to see what would happen next and what America would do for its ally, then gauge the response of Israel to the military threat coming from Syria. The two countries would watch Israel's response, checking for the latest technology and tactics used by them. By doing this they would learn the weaknesses and strengths of the equipment they sold to Israel's enemies. This was done in order to learn and counter the actions of the new technology and tactics used against Russia and Chinese allies in the Middle East in preparation for war against them in the future.

Once again, the world stood on the edge of the abyss, waiting for the next world war between two nations that couldn't get along with each other because of their differences in religion. It had been that way for thousands of years. Both sides had friends with nuclear capabilities with guarantees of support from their allies. In Israel's case, they had an extra ace up their sleeve. They would use their own nuclear weapons, if necessary, to protect their country from any threat that they deemed big enough to require a nuclear strike. This is what the world feared the most, a religious war that would escalate into a world war. The threat of previous wars had not required a nuclear option. That being said, if Israel were pushed in the wrong direction, they would use that option, if necessary, to stay alive. The question was, would this threat from Syria be the start of a war that would envelop the world? And the other question was, who would win the war?

The national news networks were already broadcasting the military move by the Syrians against Israel and, of course, both sides were blaming each other for the threat of war because of land issues. Israel was building more houses on captured property from the previous wars. Syria was claiming the land where the houses were being built as theirs. However, in reality, the fact was that all of the Middle East didn't want Israel around and they were using any excuse they could come up with to start a war to wipe out the Israelis for their own purposes. Israel, of course, was the thorn in the side of the Middle East, a thorn that wouldn't go away no matter how hard Israel's enemies tried to do it. In a sense, it was David and Goliath every time a war was fought against Israel. It was beyond anybody's imagination how Israel could win all the battles it had fought and leave the losers with less land than before the war had started. Of course, no one wanted to take the blame for losing the wars against Israel, so it had to be America's fault for their support of Israel. Maybe so, maybe not. The answer to all of this would rest in pages of history one hundred years from now.

In the meantime, the United States was actively engaged in helping Israel one more time to meet and destroy their enemy. The ThreatCon signal was changed to yellow, which meant all forces were on alert for any kind of terrorist action in the United States and its allies. NSA and CIA were all involved in listening and deciphering all intel coming through their portals, looking for signs of any hostile actions being taken. It was during this period that Syria pulled its tanks from the border area next to Israel. At this time the Scuds were pulled back a short distance from the border as well, although this time the Scuds were better camouflaged in their bunkers and buried under a foot of sand to hide them, still within range of key Israeli targets. For the moment, all the world breathed a sigh of relief.

As Israel continued to reconnoiter the area with their UAVs, their intelligence confirmed that the threats had been removed. Little did anyone know that the real threat was fifty miles further up and twenty miles further back from the border of Syria, where the real Scuds were in place, all quietly put there during the night. Unseen by the satellites and other resources of the three super powers, the first part of the plan was now in place, accomplished by the Syrians for ISIS, Al-Qaeda, and the other countries that supported the war effort against Israel, namely, Saudi Arabia, Iran, and Iraq.

As everything was considered back to normal, being confirmed by satellite photos and Israel, the ThreatCon went back to green.

Chapter X

Miguel and Lucas had been watching Diego Alvarez, after having one of the bank employees fix his account at the bank. Alvarez was completely unaware of what was going on with the money being transferred into his account. Montoya was monitoring all the computer printouts from his financial reports, which indicated that money had been transferred into the dealer's account. Now that the bug had been planted in Montoya's head about drugs being bought by Alvarez, he started paying closer attention to what was going on with the dealer's account, and he started noticing money being put in on a daily basis and always from an unknown source.

Montoya was getting angry, thinking that Alvarez was trying to build his own drug empire and maybe get rid of him in the process. He knew he had to act and act fast in order to save what he had created by working with the cartel. In the following days the police chief came around for another visit, "We've received an anonymous phone tip about some men that were killed in Nogales a few days back, claiming that you, Mr. Montoya, were involved in their death. Supposedly, they were being used as coyotes for the cartel. Do you have any idea what they are talking about?"

Montoya looked surprised by what the police chief had said to him, "I know nothing about any deaths of men in Nogales."

"I find it kind of strange that people would call in anonymously to say that you were involved in a murder committed in another town and claim that you made the call from Mexico City. I personally think it's nonsense."

"I am surprised, as well, by this kind of accusation, Chief. This, to me, is outrageous for someone to claim such a thing."

"I think it's outrageous as well. Sorry to have bothered you about this. If I hear anything more like this, I will call you and let you know. Good day."

As Montoya watched the police chief leave his office, he thought to himself there was only one other person who knew that the men killed in Nogales worked for him. It was, of course, Alvarez and if anybody could put Montoya into jail, it would be him. Montoya needed to act now or face going to prison or worse. Deciding to call some of his own men from the cartel there in the city, he told the leader of the group, "Mr. Alvarez has become a liability and needs to be terminated and never found again."

The voice on the other end of the line answered, "It will be done as you ask."

Little did they know that the line from Montoya's office had been tapped and the police chief had someone listening to all of the president's conversations on the phone. Upon hearing from the man listening to the tapped phone line about the hit on Alvarez's life, the police chief called Miguel, advising, "Just so you know, our plan is working. Montoya put a hit out on Alvarez this afternoon. Do me a favor and don't let Alvarez get killed."

"We will do our best to keep an eye on him and keep him alive," Miguel said.

By now Mr. Alvarez wasn't having any luck getting in touch with Montoya and didn't understand why he couldn't. The next day the police chief had Mr. Alvarez picked up and brought in for questioning. He showed him the photographs of the drugs that were found at his place, "How did you come to have drugs delivered to your house?"

Totally surprised by this, Alvarez had no answers for the Chief. "I don't know where the drugs came from," Alvarez said nervously, continuing to look at the photos.

"You know we have enough evidence on you that we could arrest you right now?"

"I'm telling you those aren't my drugs, I've never seen them before."

"I guess you're going to tell me you had nothing to do with the deaths of those men in Nogales, either?"

By now Alvarez was sweating and was having a hard time saying anything. "I don't know about anybody getting killed in Nogales."

"Well, we received an anonymous phone call, stating that you were involved in killing the coyotes in Nogales, is it true what they say?"

Alvarez began thinking that maybe the banker was behind all of this. "I don't know what you are talking about, as far as any murders being committed in Nogales."

Ruiz could see that Alvarez was on the verge of breaking down and inwardly smiled knowing that the rats had taken the bait. Having insufficient evidence to hold Alvarez, they let him go with a stern warning not to leave the city without telling the Chief first. Out of the building and back out on the street, Alvarez started walking back to his office. As he was making his way through the parking lot, Lucas fired his gun at Alvarez in hopes he would think a hit had been put out on him. This really scared Alvarez and he went running back into the police department building and back to the police chief. Going directly to the secretary, he begged for protection from the police. The secretary called the police chief and asked what she should do with Alvarez. The police chief, not wanting anything to do with this, told the secretary, "Tell him,

'You made your bed, now you sleep in it.' And have him escorted out."

At this point the secretary called for two officers to escort Alvarez out of the building back out on the street. By now Miguel was waiting for Alvarez to come out of the police building and get a cab and drive away. Lucas was with him, giving directions as they followed Alvarez in the cab. Arriving back at his house, Alvarez got out of the cab and started walking up the driveway when a car came by and the occupants opened up on him with their guns. When Alvarez, already nervous, saw the car as it made its way towards him, he dropped to the ground and crawled behind some trash cans to hide. Miguel and Lucas fired at the passing car, hitting the shooters and wounding the driver. The car stopped in the street and Miguel went over and checked the driver out to see if he was going to make it. The driver, seeing Miguel coming toward him, grabbed his gun and started firing at Miguel. Miguel fired once and the driver was dead. Lucas went up to find Alvarez hiding behind the trash cans, trembling like a little school girl, begging for his life. When he showed the police badge that he had borrowed from the Chief, Alvarez quit shaking so much and thanked Lucas for saving his life. Miguel came up and told Alvarez, "It's a good thing we were following you today; otherwise, you'd be dead right now. I don't think I would go into your house, if I were you; it may be booby-trapped with a bomb set up to explode as you open the door to walk inside. I think you better come with us."

Alvarez was still trembling as he got up off the ground and left with Miguel and Lucas as they drove to their hotel. Miguel had Lucas check the hotel entrance to make sure nothing was out of order. Of course, Lucas knew that Miguel was playing a game for the sake of Alvarez when asking Lucas to sweep the area for him. Waiting a couple of minutes and then coming out, Lucas gave the all-clear signal as he stood by the hotel entrance. With the signal from Lucas, Miguel took Alvarez by the arm and led him into the hotel and then to their room. As they opened the door, Lucas went in first to make sure there were no unexpected visitors inside.

Once inside, Miguel called the police chief and informed him, "Just so you know, we're safe and sound in our place. Your more than welcome to come over and interview our guest, if you wish."

"I will be right over as soon as I can," the chief replied.

In ten about minutes, there was a knock on the door and, after looking through the peephole, Miguel opened the door to let the police chief in. After walking in the Chief looked at Alvarez, still shaken up from the attempted assassination. The Chief had to turn his head to keep from smiling and giving himself away.

The Chief sat down and pulled out a tape recorder and laid it on the table next to him. With the assistance of Miguel and Lucas, Alvarez was brought over to the table to be questioned by the Chief. "Good afternoon, Mr. Alvarez. How are you doing?"

Alvarez looked at the him as he sat there, "How do you think I feel today, especially after being shot at?"

"Yes, I hear it was a close one for you. I meant, right now, how are you feeling?"

"Better now that I am safe in here with your policemen."

"That's good. I'm glad they were there when you needed them. Now, tell me all you know about the bank president and his operation."

"What would you like to know first?"

"Let's just start from the beginning. How did you get involved with Mr. Montoya?"

"It was just about three years ago this October that he contacted me to do some work for him in selling some electronic equipment to a foreign investor."

"Where was this foreign investor from?"

"Germany, I think, but there were other people there from the Middle East, as well. It seems to me they didn't understand English very well because they had an interpreter there to translate for them."

"Do you remember the name of the company from Germany?"

"No, I don't remember."

"What did they want from you?"

"They were interested in buying some electronic equipment that would transmit signals to a specific type of electronics used in guidance systems."

"What kind of guidance systems and for whom?"

"The impression I got was it had to do with something in the Middle East. I   think some kind of equipment used for jets or missiles or something like that."

"Who was the German that you met in the meeting?"

"I don't know who he was, all I know is he was an old man and he asked most of the questions, then waited for the translation for his friends. When I answered the questions, it would take a minute or two to translate it for the others there."

"How long was the meeting with the German and his friends?"

"About an hour, then we took a break. After the break the foreign men were gone, and only the German was there, talking to the bank president."

"What happened then?"

"As I had walked in from the break, he asked me how long it would take to get the electronic equipment ready to sell."

"I told him it would take a month to clear all of the hoops and get the parts together for the sale."

"How did they feel about this?"

"They seemed pretty happy to be getting it so quickly."

"Did you ever ask them about why they needed this electronics stuff?"

"I did, when I was trying to figure the timeline for delivery to them. I never got an answer to that question. They kept asking other questions about my ability to get the material and who I was buying it from."

"What happened next?"

"Nothing. I never heard another thing about it until about a month ago, from the bank president. It was then that he told me to order the parts and get them ready to travel to Germany."

"What did you do next?"

"I got the order ready and was waiting to send it out when all of this stuff started to happen."

Both Miguel and Lucas's eyes lit up on the last statement from Alvarez. Seeing this, the chief asked, "Where is the stuff you're getting ready to ship?"

"It's where I work, safe in a container in the warehouse."

"Can you take us to your office and show us where it is?"

"Yes, of course I can. I haven't received payment for it yet. I was told not to deliver the parts until I had the money."

"When was this supposed to take place?"

"From what I understand, in the next couple of days, hopefully no later than the end of this week."

"Very well, you stay here with one of my men and we will go to your office to check out this container."

"If you wish, I'll show you where it is inside the warehouse."

The chief thought about that for a moment and looked at Miguel, who nodded yes. "Why not, it will save us some time looking for it."

At this point Lucas led the way out of the room. As he walked down the hallway, he checked once again for anything out of place. Getting to the car and driving from the hotel parking lot, they headed to Alvarez's office and warehouse. Arriving at the office late in the afternoon, it was almost time to close for the day and most of the people who worked there had already left.

Walking through his office to the warehouse, Alvarez led them to the container that had the electronics inside. He opened the container for them to see that the parts were still there. Both Lucas and Miguel looked at each other and smiled. Now the problem was what to do with the parts inside the container. Taking Lucas aside, Miguel asked, "What do we do with this stuff, now that we got it?"

Lucas looked at him. "I know that we don't want to send it to Germany just yet."

Miguel pulled his phone out and took pictures of the electronic parts and sent the picture with a text to Bertrand that read, "What are these, and why do the Germans want them?"

A text came back, "Who is getting them in Germany?"

"What is the company that these are going to?" Miguel asked Alvarez.

Looking at the side of the container, Alvarez showed Miguel the address to where they would be sent. Miguel texted the address to Bertrand. In a few minutes the text notification went off with Bertrand's reply, "Stand by."

By now Lucas, who was looking around inside the warehouse, heard a noise and went to check it out. He came back a few minutes later, "We have visitors coming."

"How many?" Miguel asked.

"Five, maybe six, men with a dolly, coming this way."

Everybody looked at Alvarez, who in turn said, "We're not expecting anybody for any kind of pickup this late in the day."

By now the Chief and Miguel were making their way to the door, where the men would be coming through. The Chief grabbed Alvarez and hustled him off behind some boxes in the corner of the warehouse. He made sure that he was safe, and then instructed him, "You stay there until I come back for you; do you understand me?"

Alvarez nodded his head and hid behind the boxes and waited. By now Miguel and Lucas were in place, with the Chief making his way to the other side of the door. Finding some good cover, they all waited for the men to come through the door. With the lock being broken from the outside, the door opened and all six men walked through with a dolly, looking for a specific container. As the men stood there, the leader of the group said, "Remember, the one we want is the one that has the destination of Germany on the outside of the box."

With that, all of the men split up and started looking for the container. Thinking quickly, Lucas headed back to where the container was and switched the address on the container with another one nearby. Running back to Miguel, he motioned to Miguel to let them pass. The Chief had seen the signal as well and waited for the men to find the mismarked container, and he watched them take it out of the building, load it into their truck, and drive off.

Lucas looked at Miguel and the chief, laughing. "With it sealed, they will be surprised when it gets to where it is going."

Both the police chief and Miguel laughed at his comment. "I sure like your thinking on this one," Miguel said.

Loading the container into the back of a truck, Miguel and Lucas left the warehouse, with the Chief and Alvarez following behind in the car as they headed over to the U.S. Embassy. He took Alvarez back to the hotel room to continue asking questions about the bank president. He planned on waiting for Lucas and Miguel to come back to the hotel.

Miguel and Lucas went to the guard at the embassy, asking to see the duty officer of the day (OD). The guard called inside, asking for the OD to meet at the guard's desk.

When the OD showed up, he looked at Miguel and Lucas. "What can I do for you two?"

Miguel and Lucas showed their badges and asked to be allowed to enter. The OD obliged them and escorted them to another office inside the embassy. "Is the ambassador still here?" Miguel asked.

"No, she just left for the evening," the OD replied.

"Can you call her back? It's very important that we speak to her tonight."

"Just a moment, I'll check."

Within minutes the ambassador appeared in the front of the embassy, looking for the OD. Finding him, he led her to the room where Lucas and Miguel had been waiting for her. Walking in, she looked at the two of them and excused the OD from the room, "I'll take it from here."

Looking over the container and at the two men, she asked, "What have we here?"

"Well, to be honest with you, we really don't know for certain. All we do know is that a company in Germany was to receive this in the next couple of days, and we're thinking that it may be tied to the Middle East somehow."

Looking perplexed, she asked, "What do you want me to do with it?"

"Would you mind holding it here until the FBI comes down and gets it for us?"

"Do you think it has something to do with the President being kidnapped?"

"That's what we intend to find out as soon as the FBI gets a chance to look at what's inside."

Opening the door, the ambassador called for the OD. "Come get this container and put it in my office and have a marine guard it till the FBI gets here to pick it up. Is that good enough for you guys?"

"That will do and thank you for your help," Lucas replied.

"That's what we are here for and a few other things, of course."

"We'll call our people in Phoenix and let them know we got it stashed here for the pickup," Miguel said, as they turned to leave the embassy.

Miguel called Bertrand, "We left the container full of the electronic gadgets in the embassy. If you can send someone down to get it, it might provide some clues as what it's to be used for."

"We'll have someone down there by tomorrow to pick it up for analysis," Bertrand replied.

"That should be good for us as well."

"What are your plans down there?"

"Well, we have Alvarez talking to us. The only thing left to do is to figure out how the bank president is tied to the Middle East terrorists."

"Call me when you have more information. Goodbye."

"Will do. Goodbye."

As Lucas and Miguel left the embassy, they drove the truck back to the hotel they were staying at to catch up with the police chief and Alvarez. When they arrived at the hotel, an ambulance was just leaving from the front of the hotel. Getting out of the truck, Lucas asked a bystander, "What happened?"

"Some men tried to shoot two other men as they were coming from the parking lot."

"Were they hurt or killed?"

"No, the two men they shot at got into the hotel safely, but the shooters were shot by the security guards of the hotel."

Lucas and Miguel hurriedly went to their room and opened the door, only to see the chief and Alvarez sitting in chairs, drinking coffee and watching TV. Both saw the look of panic in Miguel and Lucas's eyes. "What's wrong with you guys?" the Chief asked.

"We heard there was shooting in front of the hotel lobby by some unknown gunmen," Lucas said.

"Oh, really! Let me call my office and find out what happened," the chief said, surprised by the news.

Miguel and Lucas were relieved to know that neither of the two men was involved in the shooting.

A few minutes later he hung up the phone and walked back into the common area of the room. Looking at Miguel and Lucas, he said, "They were looking for us, but somehow the shooters they sent shot at two other guys that just happened to be at the wrong place at the wrong time. Fortunately, no one got hurt except the shooters."

"We need to move to another place if they know we're here," Miguel said.

"The question is how do we do it without being seen by anyone?" Lucas asked.

"When do they make deliveries to the hotel?" Miguel asked.

"Usually at night or in the early morning hours," the Chief replied.

Miguel looked at Lucas, "Are you thinking what I'm thinking?"

"Yeah, I think so. We leave tonight in one of the delivery vans and get dropped off somewhere else, maybe their next stop along the route."

"You got it."

Keeping a low profile throughout the night and having Lucas and Miguel watch the door and windows, the Chief continued interrogating Alvarez till it was time to go.

"So, tell me about the drug operation the banker had set up," the Chief asked.

"The drug trade was run through Mexico City to Nogales via shipments of electronic gear from my business. The drugs would be broken down into smaller shipments and taken across the border by some of Montoya's men who lived in Nogales. In fact, the men that were found dead in Nogales were part of his operation. Pretty simple setup when you come to think about it."

"What do you know about the terrorists coming through Mexico?"

"Same idea as the drug shipments; hide them in the truck, sneak them across the border, and then they're free to do what they want. When it's time to come back, they show up at a predetermined place and the banker's men bring them back over at night without being seen."

"How much did they pay for this assistance?"

"The way I hear it, they paid five hundred thousand dollars for everything, the weapons, guide service in and out of America, and a van to get them there, plus expenses while they were in the States."

"Who was involved with this operation?"

"Near as I can tell, everybody who worked for the banker, on both sides of the border, for food and lodging and weapons, you name it. Everybody was in on it."

"What was your part in it?"

"It was my trucks they used to get to Nogales."

"Anything else you care to add?"

"No, just the electronic stuff that was supposed to be sent to Germany."

"How big is the operation he has set up?"

"Well, from what I've seen, it covers the Middle East and Germany and even in the United States. He has people on his payroll all over the world."

"Does he keep records on all of this?"

"Yes, at the bank, in the big vault. The records are in there inside a safety- deposit box."

"Do you have any idea how much money he has from all of these transactions from overseas?"

"I've no idea about that. But you got to hand it to him, it's the safest place to keep your illegal gains without anybody getting suspicious."

"Hiding in plain sight, with nobody the wiser for it," Miguel said.

Lucas looked at his watch. "It's about time to shove off."

The Chief stood up and looked at his watch. "Let's go."

"I'll go first," Miguel said.

As Miguel opened the door to the room, he looked down the hallway toward the elevators, seeing nothing. He then checked behind him to make sure it was clear in the other direction as well. By now Lucas was coming out of the room, again checking behind Miguel. With both of them seeing the coast was clear, they moved on down the hallway toward the elevator, passing it to go down the stairs of the fire escape. When they got to the first floor, they headed down the hallway toward the front of the hotel. Stopping halfway and turning left, they went in the direction toward the restaurant entrance, past the dining area, into the kitchen, and out onto the receiving dock of the hotel. They waited just inside the doors that led to the dock, watching for the delivery trucks to make their appearance. So far so good, as they waited to watch for anybody that didn't belong there. In about ten minutes, a uniform delivery truck drove in. As the man went in with the clean uniforms, the three of them crawled into the van and made their way to the front, hiding behind some of the uniforms that were hanging on the racks, and waited for the driver to return to go to the next stop on his route.

As they drove away from the back of the hotel, they sat in silence, wondering where the next stop would take them and what they would need to do to plan for their next move. For the first time Alvarez was glad to be in police custody knowing that what he had told Ruiz in his interrogation would keep him alive as long as he stayed with these three men.

Chapter XI

As Dan and John sat watching the desert below them, they caught sight of a group of ten soldiers riding in small pickup trucks that were making their way across the border into Somalia. It was a ragtag group of men, carrying their AK-47s and RPGs like they were prized possessions. Finding no one to stop them from crossing the border, the group of ragtag soldiers continued on their way toward Mogadishu, trying to hook up with the antigovernment forces of Al-Shabaab as fighters from the international jihadists were called to join the holy war against the Somali government and its Ethiopian allies.

As the trucks, loaded with their supplies and men, continued down the road a roadside bomb exploded next to the lead truck, causing it to swerve off the road and take evasive action to keep from getting hit. Within seconds, a second blast landed in front of them, causing them to stop. The second truck speeded up to be closer to the lead truck, when a third shell landed behind them in the middle of the road. Two of the soldiers were thrown from the lead truck as it was taking evasive action to get away from the shells now landing all around them. The soldiers, now on foot, ran for cover into some of the burnt-out buildings near the road. Upon reaching one of the buildings, some government soldiers in hiding opened fire on the two looking for cover, killing them instantly. Then moving out of their hiding places, the soldiers went after the two trucks with their cargo of men and supplies. With the trucks now stopped, the men, realizing they were trapped, jumped off the trucks, carrying their weapons, looking to kill whoever stood in their way. A sniper firing from a concealed position started taking out the ragtag soldiers one at a time, dropping them where they stood.

After about fifteen minutes, the fighting was over as the progovernment forces came out of their hiding places and took the ragtag army's weapons and supplies, jumping up and down celebrating their win against the dead men lying on the ground. Taking the bodies, the government soldiers stripped them of anything of value and piled them up in a blast crater and left them there to rot in the sun. In another ten minutes all that could be seen were the dust clouds generated by the trucks of the government soldiers driving off in the distance to another area to patrol.

Dan and John slowly made their way past the village by going around it and headed to the site where the attack took place. Both of them began rummaging around the area. To Dan's surprise, he found one of the trucks was still functional. Deciding to take a chance, they got it started and, seeing that it had plenty of gas, they both got in and drove away, instead of walking, through the desert, thereby saving time, in order to meet the old woman in Hargeisa. Following the road through the desert, they continued on their way through Somalia, hoping they wouldn't run into the same group of men that had attacked the insurgents earlier.

As they continued to drive through the desert, they were able to travel a goodly distance by following the road. When they came close to another town, they would drive around it to avoid detection from any groups that were operating in the area that might perceive them to be the enemy. They were able to do this for a couple days, until they ran out of gas and were forced to walk. Having no real place to refuel, they left the truck alongside the road and continued walking to Hargeisa. Continuing to travel at night, they arrived in the city in the early morning hours. Sitting in the marketplace, wearing traditional garb, hiding in plain sight, they waited for the old woman to make her appearance to sell her wares. Waiting till 9:00 a.m., they watched the merchants come in and set up their tables for food and other necessities to sell to the ones that had money. Later in the morning the sellers would start their pitches to the locals as they walked through the tables of the marketplace. They sat patiently, watching the sellers' market their goods. By now the marketplace was full of people, looking to buy and trade for what they needed. All of the men carried guns of some sort with them as they went from place to place looking at what was being sold, mostly carrying AK-47s, while others had RPGs slung on their backs as they moved around. As they sat there watching the people moving about, Dan nudged John, and, using his eyes, had John look over in the direction of another peddler setting up her business. She was an old woman, who was having a hard time getting around from the arthritis in her hands and feet. The people were pushing and shoving her around as she tried to set up her table. After being knocked down, Dan and John stood up and walked over to where the old woman was and helped her clear an area for her to set up her table. As they helped her get her meager things out to sell, they watched over her table so that no one would steal her goods. After about an hour of doing this for her, most of her wares were sold. She then started taking down her table, getting ready to leave the marketplace. Following her, they helped her get back to the place where she lived. Putting her table and the merchandise that didn't sell inside her place, they waited for her to finish her counting of the money she had made. It was just enough to buy her some food to eat for the day. Looking around her living area, Dan and John couldn't believe how sparse her living space was, with just the bare essentials to live on. While she was doing her chores of putting her table and other things away, Dan went back to the marketplace and bought some more food for her, along with some cooking pots to use. The old woman was very thankful for this extra food and pots to cook in and she thanked them and was smiling the whole time as she cooked her food.

John finally approached her and told her who they were and why they were there. She acknowledged what he had said, "Yes, I thought you might be the ones I've been waiting for."

"What can you tell us about the terrorists in this area?" asked Dan.

"They are very bad here. You saw some of them walking around the marketplace today."

"Where is their headquarters located?"

As she started eating her food, she answered, "About 50 miles from here, towards the coast, is a place called Berbera. I think this is where you might find the leader of the terrorists. This is also the place where I hear of a new prisoner is being held captive. He is not your typical prisoner, he is treated better than the other prisoners because he has his own cell and is separated from the other prisoners."

As John looked at Dan, he asked, "Are you sure about the location of this new prisoner?"

Hagath answered, "Yes, I am. I have overheard the men talking about a new prisoner being taken. They all claim he is important, he's different from the other prisoners in jail there."

"What's the best way to get there from here?" asked Dan.

"By bus, if it shows up. It leaves once a week on a Friday, which is two days from now."

With this new knowledge, John looked at Dan. "What do we do now?"

After thinking for a moment, he said, "Contact our handler and let him know what we've found out so far."

After excusing himself, John went into one of the corners to talk to the handler on the sat phone. When he was finished talking he came back and said, "The handler will set up a team to meet us in Berbera on Saturday to coordinate any and all action. They will begin transmitting once they are in place in the evening. He also told us to stand by until further notice once we get there and coordinate with the other team."

For the next few days they helped the old woman with whatever things needed to be done around her place. John could see in the old woman's eyes that life had been hard for her since her husband had died. Living in Hargeisa wasn't easy and had taken its toll on her. Still regal as a princess should be but weathered down by age and location of living, she was still a princess in her mind. She carried herself as one should. John felt for the old woman and treated her with the respect that she was due. Dan couldn't help but notice that John was bending over backwards to assist her. He smiled at what he saw, although not saying a word. He too saw the princess underneath all her age and loneliness.

Thursday night Dan and John talked about the upcoming trip for tomorrow to Berbera and what they expected to find there. The old woman, listening to the conversation, didn't say a word, knowing that she would be left behind now that the information was obtained. She moved over closer to John and asked him, "Can I go with you to Berbera?"

"Why would you want to go with us?" he asked as he looked at her.

"Because I'm old and there is nothing here for me anymore, besides, I may be of help to you yet when you get there."

John looked at Dan. "What do you think?"

Dan realized that John wanted her to go with them, not only for her assistance once getting there but, also, for her to find some peace in her life. He stood there, thinking about what she had to offer. "We cannot guarantee your safety once we get there, you know this?"

"What is safety at my age? I am an old woman now. Besides, it might do my heart some good to have something different to think about."

Dan looked at John and smiled. "I believe we may need your help in finding the prison once we get there."

John looked at Dan and whispered a "Thank you" to him.

Dan nodded his head and smiled, thinking to himself, *"Some tough guys we are, aren't we?"*

On Friday, the bus showed up in the center of the city at the bus stop. Taking the old woman with them, they boarded the bus for the trip to Berbera. Riding on the bus was hot and miserable, yet still better than walking to Berbera. About twenty miles outside of town the bus was forced to make a stop because there were bandits blocking the road looking for food and money. Searching each one of the passengers on the bus for valuables, eventually they made their way to the old woman. John had his Glock ready, as did Dan, when they started to go through the old woman's bag. One of the lookouts for the bandits noticed a cloud of dust on the horizon coming in their direction. Fearing that it was a group of soldiers he alerted the others. Realizing that they needed to leave and not having found anything of worth, the bandits quickly left the bus and loaded back into their vehicles and disappeared, letting the bus go on to Berbera. Carefully replacing their guns back into their holsters, they sat back in their seats as the bus continued on. Arriving in the afternoon, they got off the bus in Berbera and followed the old woman to a small cafe to eat dinner.

They stayed there until it was late in the evening, watching from their table the comings and goings of the people. The old woman spoke to Dan and John in whispers barely audible. "The prison is over on the west side of town, near the port. It's in a three-story building that once was a home for the king many years ago."

John got up from the table and went to get a better look at the prison to see what they were up against and to report to the team, which was coming in tomorrow, hopefully, to help get the President out of the prison. With luck they would be able to pull this off in minimum time and without incident, provided that the President was there.

Chapter XII

Sitting inside the windowless building of the National Security Agency (NSA), a young lady was monitoring the signals coming from a satellite that was picking up new chatter from the Middle Eastern part of the world. Once again, the signal was the same as the ones previously picked up, that the director had talked to Acting President Vance about. Typing down the time and length of the transmission and a rough interpretation of the message, she forwarded it to her supervisor, who checked on the date and time for verification of the message, confirming that this message was a high-priority transmission. He then wrote it into the daily log book for the day's transmissions, then sent the message forward to his supervisor, who initialed it, saying he had reviewed the message and confirmed the priority of it. The shift supervisor it forward to the director. Once he reviewed it himself, he took the message, put it in a folder, and carried it to the acting President, who was in the Oval Office with a group of kids, listening to how they won the Little League World Series the week earlier. Standing outside his office waiting to meet with the acting President, the director let the secretary walk in and tell him that something had come up that needed his immediate attention. Vance acknowledged the secretary's message and, closing out his visit with the kids, shook each one of their hands before they left the Oval Office. As they were ushered out of the office by some of the Secret Service personnel and his secretary, he waited before calling in the NSA director.

As NSA Director Dave opened the door, he walked past the secretary, who stood there waiting to close the door behind him so that they would have some privacy. Dave held up the message he had received from his people. "We got another one for you."

"Were you able to decipher it?" Vance asked.

"No, not all of it, sir. However, we got part of it translated. It reads, 'All is well and I will shortly be free.' The rest of the message is in another dialect that we think is a dead language."

Acting President Vance sat there, trying to decipher what it meant, and who had sent it. He looked at Dave. "Do you have any idea what they're talking about?"

"No, sir, we have our smartest people working on it as we speak. Hopefully, we will know more later today."

Vance looked at Dave. "Thanks for letting me know about it; let me know if you have anything new to report."

That was Dave's cue to leave and as he did so, he said, "Thank you, Mr. President, and will do, sir."

As soon as Dave left the Oval Office, Vance picked up his personal cell phone and called the man one more time. "We just received a new message. Watch and see what happens and let me know what you see."

"Will do, sir."

Hanging up the phone, he sat there thinking about when the FBI had contacted him about some messages that had been picked up by their Intel people who monitored the radio communications coming in and going out from one of the rooms inside the White House. The signals that were received and transmitted were not sanctioned by the intel personnel. In a quandary and not knowing what to do about it, they asked Vice President Vance, "How do you want us to handle this?"

"What do you mean, handle this?"

"Sir, we think the President is receiving messages from the Middle East that may be a problem for the security of the United States. If we approach the President, it may be nothing, or it may be a security breach. We do not want to tip our hand, just in case it may be a problem for all of us."

"Have you contacted the CIA to check it out?"

"Yes sir, they have confirmed that the signals are coming from Somalia and they have no one to decipher it yet."

"How about the NSA, have they been able to do anything with it?"

"Our best guess is that the language they're using is a dead language that no one knows anything about."

"So, what do you think we should do about all of this?"

"Frankly, we're not sure what to make of it, sir, but we're concerned it may affect our security, if not for the U.S, maybe one of our allies."

As Vance sat there and thought about the meeting with the NSA Director, he remembered how surprised he had been when the President had decided to go on a peace mission to the Middle East and visit the countries that were considered terrorist states and avowed enemies to Israel. He had considered his actions as brazen and a slap in the face to Israel, especially knowing that these countries helped fund other terrorist nations as well. The American people were confused by his actions and his rhetoric when speaking to the nation. His actions, in one sense, were considered conciliatory by some, while others considered them almost treasonous. Either way, the nation was caught in the middle by the actions of the President. Now that he'd been kidnapped, what should be done other than to find him and rescue him from his abductors? If found, he would be reinstated as President to continue his tenure as one of the most powerful leaders in the world, with the possibility of winning the next election for another four years because of his kidnapping, with a possibility of taking America further down the wrong path. The question that rested on Vance was what to do with the President if he was found guilty of being part of a bigger plot to destroy America or one of its allies.

The President was still the President, however, even if he was a traitor to the constitution of the country he had sworn to protect. But what to do with him if he was found guilty of trying to destroy our nation. You can't just go out and put the President in jail, or could you. What would it do to America's image in the world if he was put in jail for treason? What would the world think of America if it couldn't control one man's desire to destroy America or rule the world? Maybe it was a moot point, maybe it was just a misunderstanding by the people in the Intel world. Only time would tell if it was any of the above.

Vance, not finding any answers to his questions, went back to work by calling in the secretary and asking what was next on his to-do list for the rest of the day. She quickly told him of his itinerary and left the office, closing the door behind her, to leave him to his work. This time it was to meet with one of the Chiefs of Staff for an update on the situation in North Korea and the launching of another ICBM. Only time would tell if Vance's suspicions were correct or just a misunderstanding. Vance was hoping that it was the latter of the two.

Chapter XIII

Being able to leave the hotel undetected was a miracle in and of itself and having the answers from Alvarez was the frosting on the cake. Knowing what was going on was refreshing to all the players, instead of trying to guess at the next step in the game being played by Montoya.

The question now was, what to do about Montoya and his Middle Eastern friends. Following Montoya was easy enough, locating the Middle Eastern connection and who they were was the problem at this point. Arresting Montoya would solve only one part of the problem but wouldn't solve the greater problem of locating the terrorists who were holding the President and their intentions. That was more paramount than anything else. Finding the terrorists was the ultimate goal for them, getting the banker and shutting him down was just an added bonus.

Operating from a safe place in new location now gave Lucas and Miguel time to work out the next steps as they waited on the FBI to come forward with information on the electronic parts. Having this information would help immensely in discovering the real motive for the terrorists' plans and possibly help locate where they were. What was their game, who was it against, and had it already begun? Time was the only thing in their favor and their greatest enemy, as well. The FBI had sent a team down to look at the electronic devices at the embassy. They were trying to reverse-engineer the parts to determine what they would be used for. In the end, it was determined that taking the container back with them to

Quantico to do their work would save them time. Alvarez had an idea about their use but couldn't confirm it without seeing the rest of the electronic assembly that it would be hooked up to. The other parts needed to prove Alvarez's theory were ordered or built somewhere else in Germany, and only the terrorists would know for sure.

Miguel and Lucas had an idea about what it was intended for, but it was only an idea. Not knowing for sure was the real problem. Why would the terrorists need electronic parts and what would they be used for? Not knowing anything else, they decided it was time to go after the banker and his confederates. Up to now Miguel and Lucas had been in a defensive posture, trying to find out about who was behind all of this. Now having Alvarez with the answers gave the team an edge in this game of cat and mouse. Miguel asked the Chief, "How do you want to proceed with this?"

The Chief looked at the two men. "Let's go get the banker and make him crack."

"What about Alvarez and his game?"

"Put him in jail and I'll place him in solitary confinement for his safety, and we'll go from there."

Calling for a police car to come and pick them up was risky at best. The chief knew that he still had people that were on the cartel's payroll and would love to not only kill the police chief but also kill Alvarez for the money and much, much more. Contacting the police department to come and get Alvarez wasn't an option either. This would put their only witness in danger of getting killed by the men loyal to the cartel that worked inside and outside the jail.

"Let's take Alvarez with us on our next step of the plan. We have his information but under the circumstances, I don't trust my men to keep him alive," the Chief said as he considered all of his options.

"I agree with you," Miguel said.

Lucas looked at Alvarez. "Which do you prefer? Working with us, or sitting in jail waiting for the cops to shoot you while you're in there?"

Alvarez was quick to answer, "I'll take my chances with you guys."

"We figured you would," said the Chief.

Now that everybody was on board, they were ready to start the game again. This time bank president Montoya was in their crosshairs. Taking a taxi and going back to retrieve their car, they drove to the bank where they dropped off the Chief. Walking into the bank, the Chief went directly to see Montoya. As he waited for the secretary to show him in, he sat quietly in a chair in anticipation of the door opening and seeing the look on the President's face. Once the door opened, the Chief stood up and went to shake Montoya's hand. Montoya was surprised to see that he was there waiting for him. Trying to hide his surprise, he invited him into his office. Closing the door behind the two of them, Montoya asked, "What brings you here so early in the morning?"

"I just happened to be in the neighborhood and thought I would stop by and check to see if you knew where Alvarez was," he said as he sat down in a chair opposite Montoya's desk.

Montoya, looking at him, knew full well that the Chief knew where Alvarez was, but closing his eyes for a minute, he waited before saying, "I haven't seen him in several days now. I thought maybe you might have him."

"We did, but he got away from us in his escape from the jail. The Americans want him now and are asking a lot of questions that only he can answer. It seems that the FBI and the Border Patrol want to talk to him about smuggling drugs across the border into America and are especially interested in who he is working for."

Montoya, hearing this, went hollow inside, knowing that eventually he would be found out if Alvarez talked to the FBI. The FBI was untouchable when it came to bribes and intimidation from others. Still looking at the Chief, he said, "For your sake, I hope you find him and bring him to justice. Is there anything I can do to assist you in your search for Alvarez?"

"No, we'll find him. I just hope he doesn't fight us so that we have to shoot him."

Montoya nodded his head in agreement. "Is there anything else I can do for you?"

"No, you've been most kind. Thank you for your time."

"Not a problem, feel free to call on me anytime if you need my help."

The Chief stood up, as did Montoya, and shaking hands once more he said his goodbyes and walked out of his office. Waiting in the parking lot, Miguel saw the Chief exit the bank, and after a few seconds he honked his car horn to let him know where he was parked. He walked over to the car and got in the back seat, and they all sat and watched to see what would happen next. Turning on a small receiver and waiting to hear what Montoya would say, Miguel asked, "Were you able to plant the bug in his office?"

"Yes, underneath the chair I was sitting in."

"Hopefully, it is close enough to pick up his telephone conversations from his desk."

Waiting for the police chief to leave his office, the bank president watched from his door, making sure the Chief didn't loiter around the secretary's desk. Closing the door behind him, he picked up his phone and dialed his silent partners in crime. "I need you to find out where the chief is holding Alvarez, and I want you to kill him."

The voice on the other end of the line asked, "Just Alvarez?"

Thinking for a moment, he said, "All of them, including the Chief and his American friends."

"I get the feeling he doesn't like Americans all that much," mused the Chief from inside the car. "What do you think, Miguel?"

"Well, I've never been so rudely treated in all my life," Miguel said, laughing.

"Wait till he finds out that his Middle Eastern friends have received the wrong package. They'll probably want to kill him for that," Lucas added.

"Oh yeah, I almost forgot about that," said Miguel.

Alvarez smiled. "Wait till he hears who set him up!"

The Chief, looking at Alvarez, looked surprised to hear what Alvarez had said. Then he remembered the attempt on Alvarez's life and nodded his head in agreement.

Everybody was waiting in the car as the bank president left the building and walked to his car. Following him with a pair of binoculars, Lucas told the rest of them what was happening. With their car already running, they pulled out after watching the president get into his car and leave the parking lot. Trailing behind two other cars in front of them, the president led the team over into the poor side of Mexico City. Finally stopping in front of a dilapidated house, he got out of his car and walked up to the front door, pulled some keys from his pocket, and unlocking the door walked into the house. There was a guard inside waiting for the banker, who met him at the door. Allowing him to enter after recognizing him, he shut the door behind them.

"I wonder what is going on in there?" Lucas asked.

"It's probably the stash house for his drugs and whatever else he has going on," the Chief said.

"No, it's not," said Alvarez. "It's the house that he uses to make the meth and fentanyl for his customers. I know this because he showed me inside one time, bragging about how he has made millions cooking in there."

"What else does he do in there?" asked Miguel.

"He has a stash of weapons in there as well. You name it, he's got it in the basement."

"I was just thinking, what would happen if that place caught fire by accident?" Lucas asked.

"It would probably wipe out the whole block and the people living here, as well," Miguel said.

"We need to get inside that house to see what's going on," Lucas said.

"Yes, we do. The question is, how do we do it?" the police chief asked.

"How about we smoke them out of the building?" Miguel suggested, pointing at the roof. "You see that pipe vent up there?"

"Yes, we can block that, can't we?" Lucas said.

"With the windows covered as they are, we can get to the house and climb up to the roof and block the vent," the Chief added.

"I think I see a ladder over in the backyard," Alvarez said.

Quickly getting out of the car, Miguel and Lucas walked over to the house and finding a ladder leaned it up against the house. Miguel climbed up the ladder and, taking off his shirt, stuck it over the vent. As he quickly got back down the ladder, they waited to see what would happen next. Within minutes the house started filling with vapors from the chemicals being used to create the drugs. Next, the door opened and people came running out of the house, choking and coughing from the fumes. The first one out was the bank president with the security guard right behind him, both of them looking like they had been crying. In between the coughing and gagging, they got into their car and drove off. Pretty soon two more people came out with just their underwear on. Waiting another five minutes, the police chief called his office to report a drug house on fire and people running about outside in the yard. The fire department showed up in three minutes, with the police following them. By now the president was gone, but the others were still standing there when the police arrived. Arresting them for drug making and distribution. One of the police officers happened to look up on the roof and saw a shirt covering the vent. Finding the ladder, he went up and took Miguel's shirt from off the vent and threw it to the ground. Within thirty minutes the house was clear of the fumes and with the windows open the police went inside to check out the house. Within minutes one of the police officers called for assistance, requesting a truck to load the drugs and weapons into. All the while, Miguel, Lucas, Chief, and Alvarez waited for the police to gather everything up and set it outside on the lawn. Walking over to the policemen working the bust, the Chief asked to see the list of items found inside the house. Accordingly, the chief read down the list as follows: two big containers of fentanyl, three containers of meth, lab equipment, drug paraphernalia, and four bundles of marijuana, 14 hundred rounds of ammunition, two shotguns, three pistols and two hundred thousand dollars in cash. After seeing the list, the Chief said to the lead officer, "Make sure this material gets put into our evidence room. I will hold you personally responsible if anything comes up missing. Do you understand?"

"Yes, Chief," he replied.

"Very good, I will check your account log tomorrow on what we have here. Here, take this man, he is to be held in solitary confinement until I decide what to do with him."

The police officer saluted and took Alvarez and put cuffs on him and then escorted him to one of the police cars. From there he went back to his duties to confiscate all of the drugs and weapons that had been recovered from the house. The Chief went back to where Miguel and Lucas were standing and got into the car, "There's no need for us to stay here, we need to find the bank president and find out about these terrorists."

Now the Chief, using his cell phone, called dispatch and requested a BOLO for Alfred Montoya, the president of the bank in Mexico City. Miguel and Lucas had seen the direction Montoya took when he left the house. Getting back into their car, they started following his trail.

Montoya was running scared now, simply because he wasn't able to get his money and make a run for it. The fumes inside the house were too strong and made it impossible for him to get it. When he got into his car wiping his eyes and still coughing, he told his driver to take him back to the bank. Upon arriving at the bank, he hurriedly went straight to the vault where his private stash of money was. He opened his personal safety- deposit box and emptied the contents onto the table. Throwing the safety deposit box onto the floor, he started stuffing his coat and pockets with money. Having all of the money from the safety deposit box tucked away, he headed out of the vault and went to his office to destroy any evidence of his criminal activity.

By now the police were searching the city for Montoya, watching the airport and bus station in case he tried to make a run for it and leave the city. The banker, knowing this would be the case, took the money from his pockets and coat and put it into a small travel case which he had in his office. As he did this he pulled a wig and a fake moustache out of the case to wear. After putting on the wig and moustache he walked out of the bank past the security guards and got into another car and drove off.

Miguel and Lucas were waiting to hear from the police about the capture of Montoya, but as time went on they realized he got away. After two days of searching, a warrant was issued by the Mexican court to catch Montoya, with a reward attached. The team was stymied by the disappearance of Montoya and couldn't figure out how he did it. With him gone, they had nothing to go on in order to find the terrorists or learn their intentions.

After conversing with the police, the Chief said, "We need to look at Montoya's home to see if anything turns up there."

"We looked it over the day he went missing. What do you think we'll find if we look again?" Lucas said.

"I feel we need to find out more about these terrorists before the trail gets too cold to follow. And if it means we go through the house again, what do we have to lose?" Miguel said.

Lucas knew Miguel was right. Not knowing anything more about the terrorists was causing some turmoil in Lucas's life right now. The Chief suggested, "You guys ought to call your boss and see if anything has come up from their end. With Montoya being gone, it looks as if your part of the mission is over down here."

Lucas and Miguel looked at each other, not knowing what to do at this point, deciding that he was probably right. Miguel pulled his cell phone out and punched in the number for Bertrand. Once Bertrand answered the phone Miguel said, "The banker has slipped away from us and is on the run to who knows where."

Bertrand listened to Miguel and could hear the frustration in his voice about losing the banker. Bertrand knew of their frustration since no one in the FBI had been able to find out anything else regarding the kidnapping of the President either. "Are you guys ready to come home?" he asked.

"Not knowing where the banker went, I feel there is nothing else we can do down here."

"Well, the good news is that we figured out what the electronic parts were going to be used for."

"What's that?"

"It has something to do with jamming a guidance launch system for a missile defense setup. As far as I'm concerned, you guys did good down there. You may have saved some lives in another part of the world."

Miguel passed the news on to Lucas and the Chief. "The electronic parts we found were to be used for jamming a missile defense system in the Middle East."

"We still have Alvarez with us. He's agreed to talk to the FBI about his part concerning the drugs and electronic parts that you guys have now," Miguel added.

All at once Lucas started to feel better, knowing that their part of the mission wasn't a complete loss now, and that brought back his sense of humor and his smile. For all their effort, the Chief still had Alvarez and he would turn state's evidence against the banker.

"That is good news for all of us. Can you bring Alverez with you?" Bertrand asked.

Miguel asked the Chief about getting Alvarez to go with them to America. The Chief replied, "As long as we get him back, I see no problem in you having him for a little while."

Miguel relayed the message from the Chief to Bertrand and Bertrand told him, "There will be three airline tickets waiting for you at the airport. We'll see you shortly."

"We need to get to the airport with Alvarez and when we're done with him you can have him and do your part." Miguel said, looking at the Chief.

"Do you want the transcript from our interrogation of him at the hotel?" the Chief asked.

"It wouldn't hurt any, I don't think."

"Good, I'll have my secretary send a copy with you when you are ready to leave."

"It's too late to catch a flight for today so we'll leave in the morning, can you have Alvarez ready to fly by then?"

"I see no problem with that."

Lucas had already been thinking of things that needed to be packed, as well as the first things he would do when he got back to the U.S., and was saying, "Are you ready to go yet?"

Miguel looked at Lucas and knew he was excited about going home and seeing Amber, his wife. In fact, Miguel was missing Marissa, as well, and was quite ready to go home too. The Chief, seeing his two favorite FBI men ready to go home, smiled to himself, thinking, *"If all the Americans were like these two men, I think that the problems we have between our peoples would be short lived."*

The Chief wanted to celebrate with the two Americans and what they had accomplished by having dinner with them for their last night in Mexico City. Inviting them out to his favorite restaurant at seven o'clock was the plan for the night. While there at the restaurant for dinner, all three of them celebrated the closing of the case by drinking too much and laughing at everything that each of them said as they sat there at the table. Stopping for a minute, Miguel had to go the bathroom to relieve himself. As he made his way to the bathroom he noticed a man intently watching the Chief and Lucas as they sat there eating their food and drinking. Miguel sensed there was something wrong with the man and made his way to the bathroom and waited near the door to see what he would do next. After he had watched him for a couple of minutes, he saw the man call someone on his cell phone. He hung up after a brief message was sent. Miguel, again sensing something wasn't right, was now on full alert to what was going on in the restaurant. He started looking for other people who looked like they didn't belong there but noticed no one suspicious other than this man, who was now making his way toward the table. Miguel watched as the man reached into his coat pocket for something. By now Miguel had his gun out and was ready to fire his weapon when the man got closer to his friends. He yelled at the man to stop, which startled Lucas and the chief as they now saw the man coming toward them. Lucas saw the man's gun first and raised his gun to fire at him. The man, firing a split second later, missed his target by mere inches, and Miguel fired from behind, hitting him in the back of the head. As he fell to the floor, both the Chief and Lucas stood up. Now seeing another man near Miguel ready to shoot, Lucas fired at the second man, hitting him twice in the chest. As both men lay on the ground, Miguel checked the man nearest him while Lucas and the Chief checked on the one near them.

Everybody in the restaurant was starting to clear the area and were tripping over each other to get out. Some had been on the floor under the tables, hiding and waiting for their chance to get out of the restaurant. Lucas, looking at Miguel and seeing all the panic inside, started smiling at the people, and quipped, "Please don't leave on our account, please sit down and enjoy your dessert."

Seeing that the two men were dead, Miguel came back to the table and sat down and continued eating his meal while the other two continued drinking and talking. Realizing that he still needed to go to the bathroom he got up again, "Man, with all the excitement going on, I forgot why I got up in the first place. I'll be right back," he said as the Chief and Lucas laughed at him.

By now the restaurant was completely empty, with the exception of the three of them sitting at their table. As they enjoyed their meals, the waiter came over and asked nervously about any dessert for them. Noticing the nervousness of the waiter, they asked him to sit down with them and have something to drink. Looking around and seeing no one else was there, he accepted their invitation, sat down and started to relax with them. When the police arrived at the scene, they saw their police chief sitting at the table, laughing with his friends, so they sensed everything was all right. They had the ambulance drivers pick up the bodies and cart them out of the restaurant on gurneys. After the area was cleaned up and the bodies removed, some of the restaurant staff came back in and, seeing that all four men were having a good time, proceeded to clean up the mess left by the other diners. Once the restaurant was cleaned up, the owner came over, "It's time to close. Is there anything else I can get you before you leave?"

Lucas, looking at the owner and noticing him being nervous, laughed all the more at him, asking facetiously, "So what did you think of the floor show tonight?"

This started them all laughing again, and this time the owner smiled a little and walked away, mumbling something about how crazy the four men were at his table.

The next day, the Chief had Alvarez with him, waiting at the airport while Lucas and Miguel got their airline tickets taken care of. They eventually boarded the aircraft, and the Chief stood there at the gate and watched the aircraft leave the terminal and head out to the runway to take off. He wondered if he would ever see these two men again, at the same time knowing that if the occasion arose, he would be glad to have them back again.

Reaching Phoenix, Miguel and Lucas drove to the federal building and dropped Alvarez off with the U. S. Marshals to be locked up.

Miguel and Lucas met with Bertrand, "Anything more on the electronic parts we gave you?" Miguel asked.

"We decided they were to be used to change the security sequence for some electronic system, basically override the security system and gain control of that affected system."

"Do you know what system it was going to be used against?" Lucas asked.

"No, not yet, but we're still looking into it."

"Do you have any news about our friend, the banker, yet?" Miguel asked.

"No on that one, as well; however, we started looking into his bank and found he has been doing business with the Middle East for quite some time now. He has connections with most of the countries we consider terrorist nations."

"That's good. What happens next with the bank?" Miguel asked.

"We can freeze the accounts of the banker until we figure out what he has been doing with the countries on our watch list."

"That should slow down their operations for a while," Lucas said.

"When do you plan to talk to Alvarez?" Miguel asked.

"As soon as I review the transcript you gave me. Then, I'll go from there. No use asking the same questions twice."

"Good luck on your interrogation with Alvarez. With your permission, I would like to go home and check on my wife and kids," Miguel said.

"Permission granted. Both of you get out of here until tomorrow. Oh, by the way, you got a phone call from the police chief down in Mexico City. Evidently, the two gunmen you shot last night were part of the cartel and were upset that you and the Chief disrupted their business."

With that, both Lucas and Miguel left the building and went their separate ways to each of their homes. Miguel went home to Marissa and the kids and Lucas went home to Amber. Both of their wives were surprised and excited to see them. Each of them stopped what they were doing, and quickly looked over each of their men to make sure they weren't hurt or missing anything. They each hugged their man content to enjoy being with them the rest of the day. It was a nice homecoming for each of the families.

Chapter XIV

Acting President Vance was sitting in his private quarters, enjoying some downtime watching a basketball game. His team, the Utah Jazz, was playing against their biggest rival, the Chicago Bulls. He had come to like the Jazz from his days as a freshman at the University of Utah before transferring to George Washington University to get his law degree. As he sat there eating some popcorn, the phone in the room began to ring. One of the house staff answered, "Hello, . . . may I ask who's calling?"

After listening to the caller for a minute the staff member then handed the phone to Vance. He looked up at the staff member, "Who is it?"

"He didn't say, sir. He said that you would know who he is."

At this point, Vance turned down the sound of the game. "Hello, who am I speaking to?"

The voice on the other end of the phone identified himself as one of the investigators. "As you are aware, a message was sent from the Middle East and received and intercepted by our people. It was then tracked going to the White House via a courier and was received by the first lady. It seems that her attitude about her husband being kidnapped has changed. She seems happier than usual since receiving the information."

"That's interesting. Have you been able to find the courier for the message?"

"In fact, we have. It's one of her staff that she personally picked to be there."

"I take it you're following her movements as we speak?"

"Yes sir, we are."

"Anything else for me?"

"No, sir, except we have a bigger problem, FBI sources say they intercepted a package on its way to the Middle East via Germany that contained electronic parts for some kind of security override capability against a closed system."

"You say it was on its way to a Middle Eastern country? Do you know what country?"

"From the looks of it, it appears to be going to Somalia via Germany, sir."

"Are your guys following up on this new bit of information?"

"Yes, sir, as we speak."

"Please keep me informed on what you find. As far as the first lady goes, find the source of the information coming out and destroy it, but only after you have photographic proof and whatever else you need to seal her fate, along with her husband's."

"Yes, sir, we can do that."

"Good night."

Hanging up the phone, Vance sat there for a moment thinking about some of the international intrigue going on in the world; such as, when Syria was on the border of Israel looking like they were ready to attack and then pulling back at the last minute. He thought to himself, *"What if it was just a ruse to distract the world from what their real intentions were?"* Thinking that this may be the case, he called the FBI director at home and confirmed with him that he had received the same information. He then said, "I want you to relay this new information to the Israeli consulate on how we intercepted a package containing electronic hardware headed to the Middle East via Germany. Let them know that we have no idea what it would be used for, for certain. Send the schematics of electronics hardware to them, as well. Maybe they can figure it out."

"It will be done this evening," the FBI director told him.

Hanging up the phone, Vance turned up the TV and continued watching the Jazz get handed their butts for playing so poorly against the Bulls. Situation normal, all screwed up for the Jazz.

Within the hour, the FBI director contacted the Israeli Embassy, via a courier, with the information, and a note from President Vance, that he had been directed to deliver.

The ambassador from Israel received the message from his counterpart and, as he sat there reading the message, he didn't know what to make of it either. That being said, he picked up his phone to ask his Intel agent to come into his office to look at the message as well.

Handing the message and the photos over to the Intel officer as he walked into the office, the ambassador said, "Take a look at this. We just received this from the FBI."

The Intel officer read the message and looked at the ambassador, perplexed. "What should we do with it?"

"I don't know, that's why I sent for you."

"You remember when Syria was massing at our border not too long ago, then just pulled back for no apparent reason?"

"Yes, I do remember the nightmare of trying to get the U.N. to do something about it."

"Does the letter say what was inside the container they intercepted?"

"They think it has something to do with an electronic override system dealing with another closed electronic system. In fact, here are some photographs and the schematics of what they found."

After studying the pictures and the schematics for a minute or two the Intel officer asked, "What do we have that is considered a closed system that could be touched by our enemies?"

"I don't know, but I bet our counterparts in Israel may know. I suggest we send the message, the photos, and the schematics forward and let them figure it out. Leastwise, they won't blame us for not sending them."

"Yes, I agree. Better to be safe than sorry."

The Israeli Intel officer took the message and all the material and headed down to the secure communications room in the basement of the embassy and sent them to his counterpart in Israel, listing the name of the German company and the location in Somalia where the hardware was to be sent. Once this was completed and after it had been confirmed that it had been received, he then closed the door behind him and went about his business.

The Intel officer in Israel read the message and looked at the material as it came across the communications channel. Not knowing what to make of it, he passed the information up through his chain of command and let them worry about it.

At this point, the head Intel officer asked his secretary to send in one of his senior intel people that was familiar with electronics. Upon arriving, the secretary escorted the man into his office. The senior intel officer stood there, waiting for his boss to finish what he was doing. Finally, looking up at him, he said, "I need you to find out about this company in Germany and give me a full breakdown of what it does. See who they do business with throughout the world."

And then handing the slip of paper and the material from the FBI to him, the head Intel officer said, "I know it isn't much to go on, but we need to know about this as soon as possible."

"Yes, sir, we'll get right on it."

"Good, I'll need it to brief the Prime Minister."

With that, the man left the office. Closing the door behind him, the head Intel officer sat down at his desk. Putting his elbows on the desk and resting his forehead against his thumbs, he wondered what the information meant for the safety of Israel and her people and where to start to figure this threat out.

As the senior Intel officer reviewed the material at his desk, he picked up the phone and called his team in. They had an impromptu meeting in which they started dividing up the work based upon their technical skills, in order to find the answers that would be briefed to the Prime Minister, once completed.

Chapter XV

John made good time getting to the Berbera prison. He noticed that the entrance to the three-story building was being guarded by two soldiers posted outside the main doors, which told him that he was in the right place. Walking around the prison without being seen was not as easy as he thought it would be. Back alleys were everywhere and getting close to the prison was forbidden by the signs posted on the prison walls. The walls were guarded by soldiers walking about on top, which would prove to be a problem for any kind of rescue. The corners of the prison had small rooms where the guards would take their breaks from the heat of the day and the cold at night, having small wooden stoves inside the rooms in which to build a fire. After surveying the prison area, he headed back to where Dan and the old woman were waiting for him in the restaurant. It took a little effort trying to retrace his steps, but eventually, John was able to find his way back to them. Meeting up with them again, John confirmed what the old woman had said and added, "The guards never leave their posts until there is someone to replace them. Each corner of the prison has a small house for the guards to stay in when they're not on duty. Not only do they have the corners guarded, but they have guards that walk from corner to corner while making their rounds. From what I could see, they have an unobstructed view of the grounds surrounding the prison, which means that when we go in to save the President, it would have to be at night."

As Dan listened he mentioned, "With night-vision goggles, the team wouldn't have much problems with the guards. I think the problem will be getting inside the walls without someone noticing us. The element of surprise will be on our side and with it being perfectly timed, it should go off without too many problems."

As they talked to each other, the old woman was listening. Speaking softly, she said, "I know a place in the main area of the prison that is accessible from the ground, which even the guards don't know about and can't be seen from their positions."

John and Dan stopped talking and looked at each other, then back at her.

"When I was a little child, my father would take us here to visit the king and his children. We children would play inside the courtyard. One day we found a way out of the castle that led to one of the streets of town. We never told our fathers about it, so they never knew. We would sneak out and go see the town and would always come back the same way before anybody missed us. Would you like me to show you where it is?"

Both Dan and John smiled at the old woman. "If you wouldn't mind showing us, it would be greatly appreciated," John said.

The old woman got up from the table and led the way back to the prison, and as they walked Dan looked at John. "I'm sure glad we brought her with us."

"Yeah, me too. This old woman is full of surprises, isn't she?"

"She sure is. I'm glad she likes us. She's made our job a lot easier."

As they continued making their way to the prison, the sun was starting to go down and night was coming on. The temperature was dropping fast and both of the men started to feel a chill in the air. As they reached the prison, the old woman motioned for Dan and John to follow her. As they moved to one of the streets next to the prison, the old woman smiled. "Such fond memories from my childhood are here. I wish I could go and play one more time with my friends." The old woman caught herself, scolding, "Stupid old woman, you wish too much."

Dan and John heard the bitterness in her words as she moved along the street, headed toward the walls of the prison, hoping that her memories had not failed her in finding the hidden prison entrance.

Finding the right street along the wall of the prison was the hardest part for the old woman. It had been decades since she had played here and everything had changed, yet still remained the same. After looking for the street and finding an old landmark, she smiled at seeing something she had remembered from her past. Heading toward another street sign and looking for an old house, she smiled, talking to herself. "I may be old, but I haven't forgotten everything."

Turning in a complete circle, she smiled again and, pointing her finger in the direction of the prison, she started walking. All John and Dan could do was watch and follow the old woman as she tried to find the opening in the prison wall based on her distant childhood memories. By now it was completely dark, and the moon was blocked by the clouds in the sky. It was downright cold, and the only light there came from the fires in the guard shacks. The lights from the houses in the city were turning on one by one as it grew darker. Fortunately, the lights of the houses were not bright enough to create a problem as to where the three of them were located.

Finding the right part of the prison wall and the hidden opening went on for another hour. The old woman was getting mad at herself for not knowing where the opening was. As she cussed at herself, something caught her eye and she headed in that direction. Using her hand, she found a ledge in the prison wall that was part of a door opening. Turning to look at Dan and John, a smile of satisfaction lit up her wrinkled face. "Here it is!"

John and Dan moved up to the wall of the prison and started running their hands over the rock. Dan was the first to find where the wall gave way a little bit. Calling John over, they pushed the wall and it gave way. After moving it another six inches they were able to find a tunnel that led into the prison and, following it, they found that it went into the main courtyard.

Dan and John looked at each other, wondering if they should go further inside and see if they could find the President themselves. They decided to ask the old woman about the interior of the prison. Dan approached her. "Where are the prison cells located?"

"I will show you where they are."

Following her lead through the courtyard, they made their way past the office area and to the backside of one of the walls. The old woman was fast on her feet and was watching her steps as she made her way to the prison cells. John and Dan were following close behind her as she made her way through the maze of hallways. Stopping short in one hallway, she pointed her finger at a man sleeping in a chair up against the door. John, looking at Dan, quietly pointed the guard out to him. John slowly crept closer to the sleeping guard, pulling a knife out and holding it in one hand and using his other hand he grabbed the keys from around the guard's waist to keep them from making any noise. He then cut the rope holding the keys. Then, Dan and the old woman walked up to John as he was trying to find the key that would open the door to the cells. After a couple of minutes of searching and trying the door with the different keys, John found the right one and the lock opened with a low screech. By now both of them had their guns ready to fire. Walking past the cells, they looked into each one, searching for the President. Not finding him in any of the cells, John looked at the old woman and asked, "Is there any other place where they would keep the President?"

The old woman thought for a moment and shaking her head, "Nowhere else I'm aware of."

At this point, they headed back towards the outer courtyard and waited to make sure it was clear before heading back to the opening. As they stood in the shadows waiting, they heard two voices conversing. Pausing to see to whom they belonged, Dan saw the two men first and, motioning with his hand, pointed them out to John. As the two men got closer, one of them said, "So how was your dinner, Mr. President? I hope it met your expectations."

"It was excellent, my friend, the best I've had since the last time I was here as a young man."

"So, you do remember the times we played together as children?"

"Some of my best memories are of being here with you and our friends, playing. Who knows, when we destroy Israel for good, we shall allow our children to play together as we once did."

"That is a day I look forward to, my friend. I meant to tell you we sent a message to your wife to let her know you were okay and that all is well for you here. I will be glad when you're no longer considered a prisoner in this game we are playing against Israel."

"The codes are still good to use, then?"

"Yes, all we are waiting for is the electronic parts we ordered from Mexico to start the war against the Jewish infidels. What will happen when America finds out that you are on our side?"

"I will talk to them as I have always done. They will listen to me and follow like sheep to be sheared by the shearer. By then, it will be too late for anybody to do anything about it. What fools these Americans are, thinking that I care about them!" as he spit on the ground.

They both laughed when the President said his last remark and headed back to the jail cell. Both John and Dan couldn't believe what they had heard. Not knowing what else to do, they left the courtyard and found the opening. Closing it behind them, they went out into the night, back into the streets of Berbera. The old woman led the way back to the restaurant and then headed into the desert.

After walking a couple of miles and making sure no one else was around, Dan pulled the satphone and called his handler and waited for the other end to pick up. Upon picking up the phone, the handler waited for the message to come through. The message flashed reading, "President behind his own kidnapping. Israel is target for war. President is a traitor to America. Repeat, traitor to America. Over."

The handler, who had waited and listened to the message before confirming what he had heard, asked again for confirmation of the last part of message, "Repeat last part of message."

Dan knew this was going to happen and replied, "I say again, President part of plan for his kidnapping, he is traitor to America, Israel is target for war."

This time the handler heard all of the message completely. "Abort mission, come home, we will meet you at rendezvous point at correct time and place."

The handler sent the message up the channel for all to read. Having a recording of the message received from the team, it was sent up as well.

Acting President Vance was asleep when the phone rang, and his aide woke him up for the call. "There's a high-level conference call coming in from the CIA director."

Vance answered the call. "What have you got for me?"

"Mr. President, we have a transmission from one of our teams out in the field. Mr. President, I think you should hear this."

As Vance listened to the recording, he sat there amazed and yet not surprised by it. He asked the director, "Where is our Seal team?"

"Sir, they're on point waiting for you to give permission to go."

"Tell them to standby until further notice. I've a phone call to make still."

"Yes, Mr. President, I will tell them to stand by."

Vance put down the phone and called his private investigator. "Sorry to wake you but we need you and your team to surveil the first lady and whoever else is involved in this game. Stand by to pick them up."

"Yes, Mr. President, will do."

Vance then called his aide, instructing, "Get the Israeli Prime Minister on the phone. I need to talk to him pronto."

The aide came back in with the phone. "The Prime Minister, Mr. President."

"Prime Minister, this is Vice President Vance calling. Sorry to bother you, but we just got word that a terrorist group in Somalia is trying to start a war with you, and it probably includes what happened a while back with Syria."

"Is your Intel good, Mr. President?"

"Yes, we have our own people on the ground over there right now."

"Very well, Mr. President, we will act on your information and go from there. Thank you. We are, as always, happy to have you as our ally."

Both men knew that what the prime minister said was partially true, knowing that Israel would even take on and fight America if it felt threatened by her. Israel had no real allies, even though America, from all appearances, was on her side. Israel had known for years that they were alone in the world against everyone, including America.

Chapter XVI

Dan and John quickly made their way back to Hargeisa, riding the same bus that took them there, to Berbera. Arriving at the old woman's house, they rested for a couple of days before heading back to Ethiopia. This time, they took the old woman with them at her request. John had become fond of her through their travels to Berbera and back to her hometown. Traveling at night, they made the border of Ethiopia and crossed into the desert, where they were to be picked up by helicopter.

Arriving in the CIA field headquarters in Doha, Qatar, Dan, John, and the old woman were put up in a hotel to rest and recuperate from their journey into Somalia. The old woman was amazed at the hotel room given her and the new clothes that John had bought for her to wear, all of which were beyond her wildest imagination. Taking a bath and getting really clean, she was reminded of the time when she was a princess in her own country.

Checking on the old woman after getting some rest, Dan and John knocked on her door to see if she was ready to eat some dinner. When she opened the door, both John and Dan's jaws dropped to the floor. They didn't recognize her as the old woman anymore. She was beautiful, all dressed up and clean for the first time in years. She smiled at the boys. "Well, what did you think was going to happen?"

Both John and Dan escorted her downstairs to the restaurant for dinner and watched her as she ate things she had only dreamed of. Both of them could only smile as she went about eating and trying new things for the first time. Being escorted back to her room later that evening, she told the boys, "I hope you realize you have made an old woman happy for the first time in years."

John and Dan smiled at her and hugged her before saying good night. After leaving her in her room, they thought about the debriefing that would begin in the morning for all of them.

The next morning came too early for all three of them, but they all knew it was why they were there. They were picked up after breakfast and were driven to the CIA post, where they were escorted into a conference room. In ten minutes, the briefers came in and sat down. Each briefer was looking for different things that were pertinent to that briefer. Each of the three answered the briefers questions as completely and precisely as they could. When the briefers were done asking their questions, they left and another briefer came in. This time the briefer was wearing a suit and tie and was not one of the locals working in the compound. He introduced himself as William Berry from Washington D.C., "Tell me more about what you heard the President say when you were in the courtyard of the prison."

Dan started off first. "With the help of this lady, we were able to find a way inside the prison. After searching for the President, we heard the President talking to his "captor" as if they were old friends getting together for dinner and a game of cards. As we listened, they continued their conversation in the courtyard. It was then we realized, as they were talking, that the President was involved with his own kidnapping and that they were planning on starting a war with Israel."

Mr. Berry looked at John. "Were you there as well, and did you hear the same conversation?"

John nodded his head, yes. "Heard every word that was said by both of the men."

Looking at the old woman sitting there, he asked, "I take it that you heard the same thing as well?"

"Yes, Mr. Berry, I heard the same thing. Your President is a traitor to his own country."

Mr. Berry sat there for a moment, not knowing what to say. Finally regaining his composure, he said, "I want all three of you to fly out tonight to Washington, D.C., with me. The acting President will want to talk to you personally about what you have heard from the President while you were there."

Later that day, a Lear jet from the agency took off from the Qatar airport and flew to Germany, then on to Virginia, landing at Andrews Air Force Base. The jet stopped and, as the three of them got off the plane, a limousine was waiting for them and took them directly to the acting President in the White House. They were seated in the front office where the secretary worked, and they waited for her to show them in. Acting President Vance opened the door to the Oval Office and invited Dan, John, and the old woman in to sit down on the couch, next to his chair. In the room were the directors for the NSA, FBI, and CIA. Vance introduced each one of the directors to the three of them, who shook their hands. Then, Vance proceeded to ask about the conversation they had heard between the President and his "captor" while in the courtyard that night.

John started off. "We were able to find a way into the prison with the help of this young lady here. We decided to search the prison to see if we could rescue the President ourselves, thereby saving some lives along the way. When we couldn't find the President, we were on our way out of the prison when we heard the President talking to his "captor" about their plans to start a war with Israel. Then, they proceeded to talk about the times they played together as children and how much they looked forward to having their own kids play together once Israel was wiped off the map."

All the directors looked at each other, not saying a word and showing no emotion, and looked at Acting President Vance, who said, "Please continue."

"Well, Mr. President, there isn't much more to say, except we called our handler and told him what we heard from the President that night, and we were told to abort the mission for saving him until we got word of what to do next," Dan said.

Vance looked at the directors. "Is there anything you want to ask them yourselves?"

The NSA director spoke first. "We have some transcripts we would like you to listen to, maybe you can tell us what they are saying."

As the NSA director played the taped transcripts to the three of them, Dan looked at John and both looked at the director. "We haven't a clue as to what they are saying."

The old woman spoke up. "Will you please play it again for me?"

This time, the director hit "play" on the tape recorder and watched the old lady as she listened to the tape.

"This a dead language that I haven't heard in years. It says that the President is safe and sound and not being harmed in any way and that you will be reunited with him soon," she said.

The NSA director, amazed at the old lady, slapped another tape in the machine. "Can you translate this as well?"

This time, as she listened to the tape recording, her eyes grew big. "This one says that the kidnapping of the President is a go and will take place on his return trip from a place called Chicago."

On a roll, the director slid another tape in and hit "play." This time, the old woman listened till it was complete. "I think they are congratulating the President on getting the access codes for Israel's space-defense system."

All of the men in the room just sat there shocked with this new revelation the old woman had described to them. Acting President Vance asked the old woman, "Did they say when the attack on Israel was to take place?"

"No mention of that."

The NSA director looked at the Acting President. "Maybe this last tape will have something on it to tell us." Loading the last tape into the machine, he hit "play" and waited to hear what it said.

The old woman listened to the tape. "It says that they hate America and their allies and that they wish they could destroy America for being infidels and that they can hardly wait for Israel to fall because America will be the next to fall."

At this time, Vance said, "I thank all three of you for coming to my office. Your superiors will be in touch with you shortly."

Dan and John stood up and, helping the old woman, they left the Oval Office, passing the secretary's desk. The CIA director said, "Take a seat out here. I'll be with you shortly."

As they sat down, the secretary asked the three of them if they wanted something to eat or drink while they waited.

The old woman asked if she could have a Coca Cola to drink. The secretary got on the phone and asked for a can of Coke to be brought to her office. As the old woman sat there, enjoying drinking her Coke, the director from the CIA came out and said, "Will you follow me, please."

Setting the can of Coke down, she followed Dan and John down the hallway of the White House. John went back and grabbed the can of Coke from off the desk and gave it back to her as they walked down the hallway. This brought a smile to the old woman's face as she continued to drink it.

Reaching the elevator, they went down into the bowels of the White House. When they arrived at the communications room, they walked into another conference room with a monitor hanging on the wall. The director turned on the monitor and sat down and waited for the screen to become clear. In a few minutes, the picture on the screen appeared and they recognized that it was the prison courtyard in Berbera. The old woman was amazed at being able to see this on a TV monitor and laughed out loud.

Watching the monitor, she could see people moving all around inside the courtyard. The flashes of light indicated guns being fired at people. The old woman thought it was pretty fascinating to see and was rather boisterous about it. John put his hand on her shoulder as she watched, to calm her down. Pretty soon a helicopter arrived and landed inside the courtyard, where you could see men climbing inside the helicopter and taking off again. Then another helicopter came in and settled down inside the courtyard, and more men were picked up. Pretty soon the picture went off the screen and the screen went blank once again.

"We got the President and killed the leader of the prison. Another team was sent into Somalia, where the terrorist camp was set up, and wiped it out along with all of the terrorists that were involved with the shooting down of Air Force One. We didn't lose a man in the entire operation, which is good for our side. We figure the deaths aboard Air Force One were already a heavy enough price to pay. We found the President alive, and he is on his way back to the United States as we speak. You should be able to read the local newspapers about his release in the early edition this morning," the director said as he stood up to leave.

Acting President Vance was watching the same thing on another TV in his office while talking to the Prime Minister of

Israel over the phone. "The codes for your space-defense shield have been compromised by an unknown source."

"What do you mean, how did this happen?" the Prime Minister asked.

"We don't know all the particulars at this time. All we know is that the codes were compromised, and you need to change them immediately."

Again, the Prime Minister thanked him for letting him know about the codes being compromised. "If and when you find out more, please let us know so that we know how to protect ourselves from this happening again."

"You're welcome and if there's anything we can do to assist you from this point on let us know," Vance said, artfully dodging the last question from the Prime Minister.

Vance hung up the phone and sighed, "If they only knew what had happened, they wouldn't be so quick to thank us for letting them know about the compromise."

Looking at his Chief of Staff, Vance said, "Well, we pulled our fat out of the fire on this one."

"Yes sir, we did, and let's hope we don't have to do it again. What are you going to do about the President being a traitor and all of the people that died on Air Force One?"

"I don't know yet. Dealing with Israel was easy compared to what we've got to do with the President," Vance said, as he leaned back in his chair.

"Yes sir," said the Chief of Staff as he left the room.

At this point, Vance was deep in thought trying to figure the best way to approach the President and tell him he was under arrest for treason and the murder of the people aboard Air Force One, and wondering how the American people would react.

Chapter XVII

The Prime Minister of Israel didn't even know that America had the launch codes for his missile-defense shield and wondered how it was obtained. He called his Chief of Staff about the compromise. "We need to investigate as to how this information was known by the United States."

"Yes sir, I will get on it. Who should I turn it over to?"

"I would think that our Army Air Defense command would be able to tell us where to look to find a possible leak in our system. Also have our own intelligence people look into it as well. And have the missile defense command order their missile launch officers to change the launch codes as soon as you can before we run into trouble again."

After speaking with his Chief of Staff he pushed the intercom button for his secretary. "Please send in the Intel chief for our meeting."

While waiting for the Intel Chief to show, he sat there trying to figure out what they would talk about besides the compromise of the launch codes. He shifted in his seat as he waited for the Intel Chief to walk in, knowing this wasn't going to be a friendly meeting. The Intel Chief arrived with a file tucked under his arm as the secretary announced to the prime minister that he was here. "Send him in," the Prime Minister said as he stood up to shake his hand.

Shaking each other's hand, the Prime Minister asked the chief to sit down across from him in a chair. After talking pleasantries for a minute, the Prime Minister got into the meat and potatoes of why the meeting was called.

"As you know, our launch codes were compromised, which could have been disastrous for us in case we needed them to fight our enemies. How did this happen?"

"We're not quite sure at this point how it happened, but we do know that there are several companies involved in this. We have information of a company in Germany buying electronic parts from Mexico and having them shipped to Somalia for use against our missile-defense system."

The Intel Chief placed the file on the desk of the Prime Minister, who then proceeded to open it up and look at the pictures and statements inside the file. After he had reviewed the material he placed the file back on the desk and looked up at the Intel Chief. "Where did you get the information to start looking for this?"

"Somebody in the U.S. Intel community contacted our embassy in New York and dropped it in their laps, who in turn sent it to us a couple of days ago."

"You knew of this two days ago?"

"If you look at the original message, you'll see that there was no sign of anything other than electronic parts that were being shipped to Germany from Mexico. The organization that ordered the parts is a terrorist group working with ISIS and Al-Qaeda."

"What can we do about this, so they'll think twice before doing it again?"

"Well, sir, the Americans have solved part of the problem for us. They destroyed the terrorist training camp in Somalia and destroyed the prison where they were holding their President."

"What about the companies that were part of this?"

The company in Germany is known as Major Electronics Corporation. They do business all over the world, selling electronic parts for automobiles and aircraft to all of Europe and the Middle East. They've ventured into China and Africa and, of course, Mexico trying to set up their global reach. They pretty much sell to whoever has the money to buy. Some of their corporate vice presidents are on the Interpol watch list for some of the ways they do business and how they get rid of their competition."

The Prime Minister's eyes raised on the last point about Interpol. The Intel Chief, seeing this, continued, "Supposedly they ran into some problems in Africa with one of the leaders who didn't want to do business with them. It had to do with how much they didn't want to pay."

"And?"

"The leader was found dead, along with his family, from an automobile accident. The rest of the country's leadership, after seeing what had happened to their leader, was very agreeable after that. It seems the company didn't pay as much as they should have for setting up business in their country."

After thinking on this information for a minute the Prime Minister asked, "So how did this company get in bed with the terrorists trying to start a war?"

"It seems that the company has bought out another company called Arms Manufacturing that deals with the selling of weapon systems in the Middle East and Africa, specifically guided-missile systems and weapons that require a Global Positioning System (GPS) to function properly. Because of this buyout, the main company not only supplies the electronics for the guidance systems, but it can charge whatever it wants for them. This allows both companies to make a profit and at the same time keep the profit under one umbrella."

"So, who is this terrorist organization they were working with?"

"They are Al-Shebiib Jihadist Fundamentalist Group, which is based in East Africa. They were working with ISIS and Al-Qaeda. Leastwise, that was until yesterday, when the Americans went and wiped out their training camp, killing everyone they could find there. Supposedly, they were responsible for kidnapping their President and holding him in one of their prisons."

"Yes, I remember the newspaper articles about the kidnapping and the plane crash. Tell me, was this German company involved with this as well?"

"Nobody knows for sure, but my guess is they could have been."

"What do we do about this company now and what they tried to do to us?"

"Well, Prime Minister, we could go in and destroy the company by some interesting ways, or we can cause some problems for them financially, or we could do nothing, at least, till we find out who was behind all of this."

"What do you mean, till we find out who is behind this?"

"I think that some other country came up with the idea of starting a war against Israel and this company saw a chance to make some money off of it."

"What do you suggest, then?"

"I suggest we take out their new weapons business, and we find out which country was involved with them that started all of this."

"What have you found out so far?"

"Syria, for sure, is a main player in this and ISIS and Al-Qaeda are as well. This is all we know of at the moment."

"Do we have the capability to go after them to stop them from doing this again?"

"Yes, Prime Minister, we do. It will be a combined effort with our military and Mossad to do it, though."

"I take it you have a plan already in place?"

"We are working on several plans as we speak. Each of the teams is working out the bugs before we choose the one that we'll go with."

"Very well, keep me apprised on how it is going."

"We should know something by tomorrow afternoon, Prime Minister."

At this point the Prime Minister stood up and shook hands with the Intel Chief who took the hint that their meeting was over. The Prime Minister was surprised by the work the Intel Chief had accomplished and was impressed that a plan had already been set in motion that would teach the world to think twice before attacking Israel.

Chapter XVIII

The Seal team was waiting on the deck of the helicopter carrier ship, getting ready to board the helicopter as it completed its preflight checks and procedures. As the helicopter started its rotors turning, the crew chief was standing by with a fire extinguisher, watching for flames coming from the engine. Seeing none, the crew chief motioned for the Seal team to start boarding into the helicopter. The rescue boats were in the water next to the carrier, moving back and forth just in case they had to pick up survivors if the helicopter crashed during takeoff.

After flying two miles from the carrier, the pilot called back to the carrier, saying, "Feet wet," signifying the mission was a go for the Seal team. Flying inside the helicopter was noisy and cold and, of course, very uncomfortable for the crew and the team. The only thing that helped with the noise were the helmets that the flight crew wore for personal communications between each crew member, which had somewhat of a muffling effect. The gear the Seals wore didn't cover wearing helmets in this case, so they had to use ear protection as best they could. Some of the Seals were fast asleep as they made their way to the LZ (landing zone).

The helicopter crew used radar and GPS to find their way to the coast of Somalia. Their purpose was to drop off the Seal team at the terrorist camp, destroy it, and come home. Simple enough, in theory, if nothing went wrong. The camp was about ten miles inland from the shoreline, due west of

Mogadishu, in a little valley near a dry riverbed that hadn't seen water in over fifty years.

Flying low, using terrain-following radar and night-vision goggles, the helicopter pilots brought the craft close to the ocean, just above the waves. Hitting the first checkpoint on the coast, the pilot called back to the carrier, "Feet dry." They banked left, going south and following the coastline until they found the dry riverbed. Then they banked right and followed the riverbed through the canyon, heading west, threading their way through the canyons and valleys. Having a pair of Apache attack helicopters escorting the Seals made the job easier for the pilot flying them inland, not having to worry about any offensive or defensive threats along the corridor. Being able to focus on finding the terrorist camp, even with the latest technology, still required the pilot and copilot to use their own eyes to confirm the location of the camp.

The Apache helicopter was a flying gunship that was able to support and sustain a combat-operation scenario for extended periods of time. Their first job was to escort the bigger, unarmed helicopter carrying the Seal team into the target area. The second mission for the Apache was to provide ground support for the team as they set down. The gunship had only two men in it. One was the pilot and the other was an offensive-and-defensive crew member, who handled the weapons on board the helicopter against known targets. Tonight, it would be offensive at first, then defensive second on egressing the area. The Apache would take out any missile threat while covering for the Seals as they went from building to building looking for the enemy.

Within ten minutes the pilot, carrying the Seal team, put the helicopter down on a nearby hill. The first part of the Seal team came out of the helicopter and set up a perimeter defense around the helicopter, waiting for the rest of the Seal team to exit the aircraft. The Apache helicopter was flying top cover just in case the Seal team or their helicopter got into a jam. The Seal team would do most of the work once on the ground. Having been briefed as to how the compound was set up, the Seals practiced daily for a week getting the tempo of the mission down pat. Once that was done, they then practiced it at night for just this type of situation. Each team member had a specific task to accomplish with one other man as backup, just in case.

Being dropped two miles away, the team started hiking to the camp. Within an hour the Seal team was set up and waiting for the Apache helicopters to make their appearance, their job was to take out the guard towers where the automatic weapons were. The Seal team was waiting in the dark near the fence line for the first explosion from the rockets being fired from the Apaches hitting their targets. The first explosion would wake up the terrorists inside the camp, with the Seals positioned to meet them, they would catch them in a crossfire of bullets.

The Seal team leader called on the radio to the Apache pilot, "Ground force set and waiting for fireworks. Be advised north tower has a machine gun in place."

The pilot responded, "First target to be taken out."

The pilot brought the helicopter in low and fast, firing rockets at the north tower. In a second, the north tower was gone and smoking as the helicopter completed its first pass over the compound, while the second Apache flew top cover for his wingman.

The explosion woke up the terrorists inside the camp and, as they came running out of the buildings, the Seals, who had booby-trapped the doors, watched them get caught in the explosion of the C-4 packages. The ones that were able to get out of the buildings were cut down by the Seal team that was in place waiting for them. The terrorists started to group together, trying to fight back against their unknown assailants, not knowing where to shoot first. The helicopter came in again and started firing missiles into the buildings that the terrorists were holed up in. Making another sweep across the compound, hitting the biggest building in the center, the secondary explosions from it told them it was the terrorists' armory that held all of their weapons. Within ten minutes the camp was on fire and all of the terrorists were either dead or hiding out in the desert. At this point the Apache, flying top cover using infrared sensors, continued firing on the terrorists that escaped into the desert. Surveying the compound and finding no one alive in the camp, the Seal team leader called for the helicopter to come and get them at the rendezvous site. Making their way to the LZ, they boarded the helicopter, with the Apaches flying escort back to the coastline of Somalia. Once hitting the coast again, the pilot radioed to the carrier, "Feet wet and mission accomplished." Within thirty minutes they were lining up on the subdued approach lights of the carrier and coming in on approach. Within forty minutes all three helicopters were sitting on the deck of the carrier, and the men were now leaving the helicopters, smiling and giving a thumbs-up sign that the mission was a success.

Lieutenant Johnson, who was in charge of rescuing the President, was pleased that the raid to get the President went off without a hitch and none of his men were hurt or killed in the process. This was considered a good mission with a quick egress out of the courtyard of the prison. The assault surprised the prison warden, who had little time to set up any kind of response to the attack. Realizing that there was nothing to be done to protect the President, Assad escaped through a hidden passage. The guard shacks on each corner of the prison walls were taken out first so that the top cover for the helicopters landing in the courtyard was protected by part of the Seal team. Another set of Apache helicopters flying cover near the prison kept the Somalia terrorists from getting close enough to be a threat to the operation.

Grabbing the President only took a matter of minutes and, half walking, half running, the team loaded the President onto the first helicopter with the designated team members providing security for him. The helicopter carrying the President was flown out to sea toward a helicopter carrier being escorted by one of the Apaches used by the marines for such missions. Landing on the carrier, the President was met by the captain of the ship, who shook his hand and escorted him to the bridge of the ship into the captain's quarters. The doctors aboard the carrier examined him and were surprised and didn't know what to say, seeing how healthy he was for having been in a prison for over a week.

The President had been in his cell when he heard what he thought was an explosion that rocked the prison. Being confined to his cell, he wondered what all the noise was. As the outer door of the jail cells was blown open, he saw the guards fall as they went to fight the intruders that were coming into the area of the cells. By now the President knew what was going on; the Seals were there to rescue him. As he sat there waiting, he wondered how they knew he was there. The plan that had been used to kidnap the President must have underestimated the intelligence agencies' ability to do their job.

Once back on board the helicopter carrier, he began acting as the President of the United States, shaking everybody's hand that he met and thanking everyone for his rescue. With an armed guard of marines to escort him all around the ship, only the ship's captain and his executive officer (XO) knew that he was a traitor. They had received word from naval intelligence about it when the Seal team was brought aboard. Each member of the Seal team knew it as well and played their part with success in the rescue. This rescue was more for show to the world that the kidnapping of the President would be handled with brute force and all who participated in it would be given swift justice for their part in it. For the lieutenant, knowing his commander in chief was a traitor and was above his pay grade, right now his only concern was about his men and that they were safe once more aboard the helicopter carrier.

The President was taken by a Harrier jet and flown to a bigger carrier to be taken by a C-2 Greyhound aircraft from there, landing in Germany for a complete physical at Ramstein Air Force Base. After a day of being in the hospital, a Learjet flew him back to the states, where he was met with cheers and reporters, all wanting to ask him questions about how he was treated while in prison, how he kept himself optimistic while in jail. Waving to the crowds that he met when landing at Andrews Air Force Base, a press conference was set up to answer the questions everybody had for the President.

The President played his part well as he thanked the greatest military in the world for rescuing him and saving him from the terrorists that he claimed were intent on killing him. He was crying tears as he said this and, of course, the American public believed him.

As Vice President Vance watched all of this inside the White House, he smiled to himself, knowing that the President was one of the best actors that had ever graced the stage. He was waiting for the President to go through another complete physical at Bethesda Naval Hospital before heading back to the White House to take over his duties as President. Of course, his family was there with him once he had landed in Germany and were asked how it was to have their daddy home and/or husband. For the next fifteen minutes of fame, the free world was caught up in all the excitement of the President and his ordeal of being held a prisoner.

Vance knew that in a short time everything would go back to normal. The people would go back to loving him or hating him as he made decisions that would affect their world. But for now the world adored him as a human being for having survived the ordeal. Then would come the task of doing what needed to be done to keep America safe, the job of bringing to light the part the President played in his own kidnapping. How would America perceive all of this? Only time would tell and only time would see if America could handle it. What would he say when all of this was brought out by the different directors of the Intel community? Some would say it was a witch hunt against the President, others wouldn't be surprised by it at all.

Vance knew that in order to protect the United States he had to walk softly on what he knew to be the truth about the President of the United States, knowing that he was a traitor who tried to set up one of our allies in the Middle East for a final war. How would America look to the rest of the world when this came out? What would Israel do upon learning of the actions of the President? For Vance, there were several ways of handling this issue. The first one was impeachment, the second, pretend it never happened and lie to the American people in order to protect them, the third was to get rid of the President by termination, i.e., death. Of the three choices before Vance, all would have an impact on the world to some lesser or greater degree. Vance knew he would either be a villain or a hero, depending on the individual American's thoughts. This he knew, he couldn't change the outcome, no matter what choice he made. In this situation, it was a no-win solution for America. Vance thought to himself, *"Why couldn't the President have died in the rescue attempt?"* That would have solved all the problems for him.

After recuperating for a week in Camp David, the President was back to sitting in the Oval Office, in the chair only he could sit in. After the press had gone from taking pictures of his first day back in the office, he smiled, thinking that he had gotten away with not being caught and almost destroying Israel. He was now thinking to himself how he could tie up some of the loose ends, the people and companies which had been involved in trying to take out Israel.

Vance was wondering how to approach the President on what he knew. As Vance drove through the front gate of the White House, he had with him all the information to show the President the details of his involvement with the terrorists and the attempt at starting a war with Israel via Syria. None of the directors from the Intel arena were with Vance on this trip. He wanted to see if he could convince the President to step down on his own accord. After meeting him at the front door of the Oval Office and shaking hands with him, the President offered the Vice President a chair. Graciously accepting the offer, the Vice President sat down and laid out the paperwork from his folder containing the information he had on the President. Looking confused he smiled. "What's this?"

"You need to read it, Mr. President," Vance said.

The President picked up the first paper, showing a list of transmissions received from the terrorist group that had been intercepted by NSA and translated into English. As the he continued to pick up each piece of paper that was laid out before him on the desk, he started getting red in the face from all the information he had in front of him. "What is this crap!?" yelled the President.

"Well, sir, this information has been confirmed by the NSA and the CIA that you were involved with the destruction of

Air Force One and you are responsible for the deaths of everyone aboard. Not only that, we have proof you were involved with giving away top-secret information to a known terrorist group to use against Israel. This, Mr. President, is your opportunity to resign and never come back into politics."

"Why would I do that? This is nonsense!" he said arrogantly.

"Because if you don't and this is leaked to the press, it will destroy your credibility and your family as well."

"Are you threatening me? I'm the President of the United States! You can't talk to me like that."

"No, sir, you are a traitor and a murderer, and here is the proof," Vance said as he pointed to the paperwork on the table.

The President was livid at the accusation made by Vice President Vance. At this point, he ordered Vance out of the office. "This is a whitewash and a smear tactic so that you can become President."

Realizing that the President wasn't going to take the offer, Vance left the office and headed to the FBI director's office and told him what had happened. "He won't leave without a fight."

"Did you expect anything less from him? He is a very powerful man with plenty of support from his friends in office. Leastwise, you gave him the opportunity to do the right thing for his family. Too bad he didn't take it, for his family's sake."

"What do we do now?"

Not knowing what to say at this point, the director said, "I'll take it from here."

The FBI let it slip out that the first lady had been in contact with her husband while he was in Somalia, and the way they communicated was through a person on her staff. When asked by the press about this communication process, she denied all of it, feigning no knowledge about it. When the person who was the messenger was charged with aiding and abetting the terrorists, the President's house of cards started to fall.

The President claimed he was not aware of any of this. That's when the tapes were released from the NSA about the conversations that had been recorded, implicating the President in all of this. His reply was that it was a smear campaign meant to destroy his credibility with the American people. The two houses in Washington, D.C., decided a special prosecutor was needed to investigate the accusations against the President. When John and Dan were brought in to testify about what they had heard and seen, both used the President's own words against him about Americans being like sheep being led to be sheared. This was the final straw for the President, who up to this point had friends but now found himself without them.

After the information was proved correct, the two houses decided to impeach the President on two counts, the first being treason and the next count for the deaths of everyone aboard Air Force One. After the court trial was complete, which was over a period of three months, the President was found guilty on both counts. The nation, who once thought the President was a hero, saw him as he truly was, a traitor and a murderer. His wife was also found guilty of treason and murder as well for her part in the plan to kidnap the President. The general public wanted them put to death for treason and murder, but, as they say, cooler heads prevailed. For just a moment in time, the President and first lady were really scared that they would die for their crimes.

After being found guilty of killing all the people on board Air Force One and of treason against the United States, and for their part against Israel, the President and the first lady would go down in history as being the only President who went to prison for life, along with his wife. He would lose his pension for being President, and all of his assets were frozen, never to be used by him or his family. The President and first lady would also lose Secret Service protection for themselves and their family, who would be sent to live with their nearest family members in relative obscurity. This President would not be remembered for anything other than being a traitor to his own country. Being given the opportunity to speak in his own behalf he continued to say that he and his family were innocent of being murderers and traitors. The press corps who covered the news briefing were given the opportunity to ask questions to the ex-President and his wife. One of the people with the reporters raised her hand and asked, "You don't know me but my husband was the pilot on Air Force One. I would like to ask you; how does it feel to know you killed people that were willing to die for you because you were the President?"

Hearing this, the ex-President stood there, flat footed, for the first time not knowing what to say. The reporters then realized that the man and his wife were guilty of the horrific events that had transpired.

Being sent to Florence, Colorado, to serve their life sentences in a maximum-security prison, the President and first lady wouldn't be allowed to be with each other. He and his wife would be basically in solitary confinement, separated and alone, for fear that the other inmates would try to kill them. Because of this, they would never see the light of day again or, for that matter, each other.

The ironic part of this whole thing was that the President and his wife thought they were better than the people they served. And now they will be served by people who will oversee their every need while in prison, the guards and support staff; and they will know that the only way they will ever leave the prison is when they are dead.

Chapter XIX

The Prime Minister of Israel watched all of this in total disbelief and couldn't understand why the President would have acted this way. Connecting the dots, it then dawned on him that the President was a believer of Allah. The hatred of Israel that the President had, only served to fire up the Prime Minister to act against the groups of people who were part of this plan. For Israel, it wasn't about being covert; it was about teaching the world a lesson of not messing with Israel in any way. The Prime Minister gave his permission to go forward to each team that had been slated for their parts. He also gave each group permission to use whatever force was necessary to pursue and complete their missions.

With the plans in place, each Mossad team went about their business, using regular troops who had trained with them to complete their missions. One team was sent to Germany, another team sent to Mexico, and the last team was sent to Somalia, there to meet the other teams before going into Syria. Each team had a mission to perform and that was to take down the organizations that allowed this to happen.

The first to strike was the team landing in Mexico as tourists taking in the sights of Mexico City. The intel they had gathered showed that the electronics company had shipped the parts to Germany, then to the terrorist camps in Somalia, was located in the city. Finding the company was easy and, after checking it out, they found that the owner of the company had disappeared and hadn't been seen in quite a while. Not knowing where he had gone, the mission was aborted and the team now turned their attention to the bank that had been involved in setting up the money for the transaction. Their Intel had shown that the bank was the connection between the electronics company and the terrorist organization that had wanted the parts.

Searching for the bank owner was another exercise in futility as well. When they discovered that the banker was gone, they sat there in the cantina, trying to figure out their next move. They were stymied by not being able to exact their revenge on anyone. Having received intel from America confirmed information from their own sources as to which cartel was in on the operation used by the terrorists. They decided that to save their mission they would go after the cartel. This was the easy part of the hunt for the team. But finding the cartel would prove to be harder than they had planned. Working through the street corners, looking for the drug dealers, and then following the right one proved to be harder than they had thought. After a few failed attempts at following the drug dealers, they got a break on the third attempt, when the drug dealer met his supplier, needing more drugs to sell. Following the supplier to his source, they were now in a position to wreak havoc on the cartel. Once the team had located the cartel operation center in Mexico City, they started making plans on how to dismantle the cartel. Now it was just a matter of time for them to carry it out.

They worked their way up the food chain to find the drug distributers, then going from there, they started looking for the safe houses where the drugs were manufactured for sale and distribution. Finding one house already destroyed by a fire, they continued looking for the new places of business for the cartel. Once they were found, it was a matter of setting some charges around the gas heater, with the pilot light out and with the gas still on. Not wanting a public backlash, the team cleared the workers out of the houses, leaving the soldiers dead inside and then detonating the small charge inside the houses. The houses burnt down in less than ten minutes flat because of all the chemicals inside. After finding one of the soldiers outside one of the burning houses, they coerced him into telling about the main route into the U.S. and all the suppliers used for the distribution of drugs and the different safe houses the cartel was using. Following his lead, the team wiped out the drug dealers, the suppliers, and the drugs themselves. The local police couldn't understand why all the dealers and suppliers were dying all around their cities, not that they were complaining about it. The deaths brought a new concern to them, that being a dealer or supplier could get you killed; that is, if you got caught doing this. It was irregular not to have somebody claiming they were taking over.

The team followed the trail all the way into the United States. They took out all of their sellers and distributors throughout America. All of this was sanctioned by the FBI and the local ICE personnel from DHS. From the viewpoint of the DOJ, it was helping get rid of the trash on the streets all through America. And the Israelis were willing to do their part in settling the score.

When the banker read about his drug houses being burnt to the ground and his cartel being dismantled, he knew that it was a matter of time before he would meet his own fate as well. Not feeling so comfortable, he now decided to run and leave the country and hide. His only option was to head over to the Middle East and find a place in one of his own companies that he had helped create. What he didn't know was that Mossad was now looking for him, and not just anybody was trying to take over his drug business.

The police chief was amazed at how many drug houses were being burnt to the ground just in Mexico City alone. When the destruction started going up toward Nogales, he knew something was going on. However, his confidential informants weren't saying anything about a new gang coming in. Nobody on the street had any idea who was dismantling the cartel one piece at a time. All they had was a body count of drug pushers being found dead, and the live ones were turning themselves in to keep from being killed. When the interrogation of the drug dealers was completed, the chief had more information than he knew what to do with as to what drugs were being sold on the streets and who was providing them.

The chief contacted the DEA about the information he had received from the drug pushers and let them sit in on some of the briefings that were given to the Mexican police when it came time to raiding a building or a street corner. He had a crazy idea for a moment that maybe Mexico City would become clean from drugs since all of this was happening, if even for a short time. Whoever was doing this was doing Mexico City a favor by cleaning up the streets. As the chief of police, he knew he needed to consider the murders of the pushers and suppliers, but it would take some time to figure it out, as to where to start, and from what he could tell, no civilians were getting hurt in the process. Yes, sir, it would take some time to look into this, for sure. But for now the paperwork was piling up on his desk and needed his attention. For the chief, it was matter of priorities.

Chapter XX

The second team that went to Germany was sent in to locate the arms factory that had built the final electronics package with the parts from Mexico used in the missile-guidance systems which would have been sent to Syria.

Pretending to be foreign investors from the Middle East looking to buy certain items that were considered questionable, two of the team members made reference to being interested in buying certain equipment that would benefit their cause against their common enemy. They were introduced by the salesman in a sales meeting to one of the vice presidents of the company, who thought he was meeting with terrorists who wanted to destroy Israel. He was more than happy to sit down with them to discuss their questions and concerns when it came to buying the equipment that the company sold. In a briefing about what the company does and where and who it does business with, the vice president alluded to their arms company in Saudi Arabia and showed them some of the arms they had sold to their friends in the Middle East. The vice president, in fact, bragged about the company's ability to move certain products to wherever it was needed in the Middle East, which was made easier due to its connections with the surrounding countries. Claiming to be impressed by what they saw and heard, they told the vice president they needed to make contact with their superiors to figure out how their company could best assist them. They begged off buying anything until they contacted their boss. In the meantime, they would set up another meeting with them as soon as they could, once they got word from their superiors. This meant they would need to fly back to consult, promising that they would return.

Following up on the intel from the company, plus the briefing they had received before they left Israel, the team ended up in Saudi Arabia in the small town of Sakaka. The factory was located in the center of town, in the north central part of Saudi Arabia, which was close to the border of Iraq and Jordan. It was an ideal place, without a lot of problems for the company, for trafficking whatever kind of hardware or anything else they chose to transport to the enemies of Israel, simply because of the proximity of the border with the neighboring countries.

After finding the arms company in Saudi Arabia, the team slowly filtered into the town by driving the same road the company took to deliver their wares. When all of them had reached Sakaka and positioned themselves as workers, they waited for the right time to do their work. Their goal was to make it look like an accidental explosion dealing with some faulty equipment inside the plant. Some of the men on the team were assigned to watched the trucks as they came in and out, to determine the driving schedules in order to maximize the damage to the plant.

With this thought in mind, they watched and waited for the trucks to come into the main plant's loading area, ready to be loaded for their next trip. The local workers loaded the trucks at night in the early evening so that the drivers were ready to go first thing in the morning. As the trucks sat there overnight waiting to be driven, the team came and planted charges on each of the trucks inside the trailers, then made their way inside the building to plant more charges there. The plan was that it had to look like one of the trucks caught fire and exploded with a full load of fuel and weapons inside the trailer. From there it was to spread to the other trucks because of their close proximity to each other and then spread throughout the plant, looking like a firestorm being unable to be stopped.

It all worked according to plan and then some. Once inside the plant, as they started to plant the bombs, they found bomb-making materials used for building IEDs (Improvised Explosive Devices) and VIEDs (Vehicle Improvised Explosive Devices) inside the main area of the factory. Setting the charges next to the bomb-making materials, the team hoped to cause a secondary explosion that would rip the plant into two pieces and burn part of the town as well. The news would report it as a tragic accident brought about by poor safety practices. The furnaces inside the plant they used to shape the charges were operated by natural gas, and with the gas going through the building, the explosion would be enough to destroy the whole complex. The team leader figured that the detonations from both ends of the building would be enough to destroy the plant and part of the city as well.

As the team drove away from the city, the team lead looked at his men. "One less problem in the Middle East for us."

The explosions rattled the town and the people that lived there ran to get away from the explosions and the subsequent fire in hopes of protecting themselves. The Saudi Arabian government couldn't believe it when the whole town was wiped out by the fire resulting from the explosions at the plant. After sending in a team of military inspectors to look over the mess created by the explosions and fire, they couldn't tell what started it because of all the damage.

The team went back to Germany and after setting up an appointment again with the same vice president of the company, the two men said that they were ready to buy from them. The vice president looked rather sheepishly at them.

"We are not going to be able to fill your request at this time or in the near future because it seems we've had a terrible accident at the complex and will not be able to do anything for quite some time, leastwise until they rebuild the plant."

Being upset after hearing the news, the two men wanted to talk to the company president about their parts order not being filled, the vice president took them to see him. Once again, the president apologized for any inconvenience the accident had caused concerning their needs. Only leaving after they were promised that when the plant was operational their order would be the first filled.

As they left the company grounds, they waited till evening before coming back to watch the traffic leaving the plant headquarters. Finding the president's car, they followed him back to his place. Later in the evening as the president settled into his nightly routine at home, the two men went up to his door. After ringing the doorbell, they waited for him to answer the door. Recognizing the two men he had met earlier, he asked them to come in and offered them a drink. As they visited, one of the men slipped a micky into his drink. Once the president was out, they carted him off to an abandoned warehouse. When he finally regained his senses, he found himself tied up sitting in a chair with the whole team standing there watching him, and for the first time he realized he was in trouble. The team leader slapped him before he began questioning him to get his attention. "Who are you working for? And before you answer, remember that if you don't answer truthfully you may not be going home tonight."

The president, knowing this was serious, closed his eyes and with his head bowed said, "There is a consortium of nations where the terrorist groups meet together to discuss ways of getting rid of Israel, with the common goal of killing all of the Jews."

"Yes, yes, we know this. We want to know who is in charge of this group," the team leader said.

"I don't know who is running it. It was before my time of becoming the president of the company."

"Where do they meet?"

"It's usually in Iraq, during the summer months."

"How often do they meet?"

"Twice a year. In fact, they have a meeting coming up next week in Zurich, Switzerland, this time."

"When and where?"

"At one of the banks that handle offshore accounts for their depositors. The name of the place won't be known until the day prior to the meeting. All of the players will be in Zurich, waiting for confirmation of place and time."

"Are you to be there as well?"

"Yes, our company represents the vested interests of a group of companies that are united in destroying Israel. They also provide the material and means to further the cause of the terrorist groups and their host countries."

"We will be attending your meeting with you."

"That is impossible. You will be found out before you get there and killed!"

"Not if you tell us where the meeting is first, and we go in your place."

"That's impossible, simply because I'm not you and the only way into the meeting is with an invitation and three security checks in the process."

"Yes, I understand, but either way we will be there to assist you in this meeting."

This didn't sit well with the president, and the leader of the team could see it in his face. Thinking for a moment, the leader said, "I see that you're not excited about us being there with you. This I can understand. The alternative is to kill you here and now and then go on from there."

The president thought on this for a moment before answering, "You are right. I will work with you."

"Consider this, you will have security with you the whole time, at no cost to you. That should be of some comfort to you," the leader said, a smile spreading over his face.

The leader had one man stay and watch the company president as he gathered the others around him. They started discussing their next step as to how to let their bosses know about the meeting that was coming up and how they wanted the team to handle it. He sent a message via a satphone to his supervisor about their meeting with the president of the company and also telling him about the next meeting with the consortium in a week. The leader asked for instructions on what to do. Standing by and waiting for further directions, the leader went back to his team and asked, "How do we want to handle this if it's a go? Do we follow the president to the meeting?"

"How about we take out the whole group of people while they are in the meeting?" said one of the team.

"That wouldn't stop what they're doing," one of the others said.

Another spoke up. "Why don't we find out who is attending the meeting and take out their companies one by one."

"That may take too long and cost us manpower we don't have," said another.

As they were discussing this, a message came through to the team lead reading, "Find out who's attending and send us photos of them, if possible, we will go from there."

It wasn't what the team leader had expected but, following the rules, they would do as they were asked by their supervisors.

Waiting a week for the meeting to happen gave the team enough time to set up by having the cameras and the team in place. The company president had complied with the team, under threat of watching his family get killed in front of him and then being killed afterwards. The leader and the president were in Zurich, waiting for the message advising where the meeting was to take place. The rest of the team was waiting to hear from their leader once he got word. As they waited in their cars, all were quiet. Each of them knew what to do once the plan was put into action, that is, get pictures of the players and then get rid of the company president.

Once the message was delivered to the company president, he showed it to the team leader, who in turn called his teams and let them know that the meeting would take place in one of the local banks that worked with foreign investors, located in Zurich, Switzerland. Having the address, the teams made their way to the location of the bank and waited for the rest of the people invited to make their appearance. As they watched from their cars, all the while taking pictures of anybody that they felt looked the part, they could see all of the people who entered the bank. In about two hours, the people walked out of the bank and the team started taking pictures once again to confirm the first pictures. Once this was done, the team leader was waiting for the company president to come back to his hotel room. One of the team watched him as he came out of the meeting and followed him back to his hotel room. When the president got to his room, the team leader had him sit down in a chair and make himself comfortable. With the president seated, the team leader, using a syringe filled with arsenic, stuck him in the arm, "You won't feel a thing from here on."

As the team leader packed up his stuff and left the room, he promised the company president that his family would remain unharmed because of his cooperation. The president smiled and closed his eyes for the last time. From all aspects, his death would look like a heart attack and would be reported as such. The family would claim the body and bring it back to be cremated, his ashes set on the mantle in a beautiful urn.

By the end of the week, the photos had been run through facial-recognition software and were being identified by Israel's intelligence services. It would take several days to go after more intel on the companies and countries they each represented, but it would get done. Having a list of targets and names of the people meeting in Zurich within two weeks was a major accomplishment for the Israeli intelligence services. The Prime Minister had to decide on what would be the best way on how to handle the list of names and who they represented. Calling his cabinet in for a special meeting to discuss the list, no one could make up their mind on how best to exploit the information for the Zurich gang. Finally reaching an impasse, the meeting was adjourned and everybody went back to their offices. The Prime Minister was feeling frustrated with no decision being made by his cabinet members. The senior intelligence chief, who had been sitting in the back of the room, watched as everybody was yelling at each other, fighting for their opinion to be chosen. He stayed until everybody was gone from the Prime Minister's office, and as he rose to move closer to the Prime Minister, he could see that the man had a headache, so he asked the secretary for some aspirin. Offering him the pills and some water, he said,

"I think I have a solution for your problem with the Zurich gang."

"Oh, pray tell, I could use a good idea that will work. What is your idea?"

"Well, I was thinking that if we could find their bank accounts, we could siphon the money from those accounts and destroy their companies from within. It would also destroy the backbone of the terrorists and they would implode upon themselves."

As the Prime Minister thought about the idea posed by the senior Intel specialist, he smiled. "Do we have the capability to do what you suggest?"

"I think with help from our friends in the United States, we could do it."

"How long will it take before we see results?"

"It's hard to say. I will know more about it once we talk to our friends across the sea and see how they do it. That is, if they share with us what they know."

"Do you have any Idea what they will want from us in return?"

"We will offer them all of the information that we find in return for the same from them."

"I think my headache is going away now," the Prime Minister said, smiling.

It was a known fact that when the United States went after a known terrorist, when it came to tracking down that person, they not only went after that individual but they went after the money trail and everybody connected to it. The Americans had turned it into a science, doing their intelligence this way. Not only did they get their man, but they also got his friends and their friends as well. And on top of that, they would freeze the money of the company or country from ever being used again and, in some cases, use their own money against them. The goal for the Americans was not only to take the head off of the snake but also the next head as well. This way, the next leader would think twice before accepting the job, knowing he could be the next one killed. The goal had always been to stop the terrorists in their tracks, both financially and militarily.

The Prime Minister left the details to his senior intelligence officer to contact the Americans and ask for help in finding the money and the best way to do it. Within days after requesting their help, the Americans agreed to support the Israelis by sending people over to assist in finding the computer systems and money records. Using technology from the CIA and Israeli intelligence resources, the team was able to find fifty percent of the bank accounts of the terrorists within a short amount of time.

Chapter XXI

The computer team was made up of two forensic computer specialists from the CIA and two computer specialists from Israel, who were computer geeks that thrived on the challenge of breaking into computer software and scrambling the computer systems. The American team members were Bill Jenson and Robert Sorenson, both of whom had graduated from the Massachusetts Institute of Technology (MIT) and had worked together for years on several cases that required their expertise as needed by different agencies within the DOJ. Their goal was that once the money was found, they in turn would follow it to determine where it went and how much of it went there. Between the two MIT graduates, they were able to figure out where the money was coming from in an operation run by the syndicate in three different countries.

The two Israeli computer specialists were Benjamin Schnitzer and David Sienski, both being graduates from the local university in Israel. They had worked in different areas in computer programming until their hacking skills had been discovered by Israeli intelligence and were put to use against anti-Israeli businesses and countries. Working together they were able to crack some heavy-duty firewalls to get into the computer system used by Iran for their nuclear facility operation.

All of their reputations preceded them as they started working together to try to solve this new problem. The Israelis were able to find a crack in the firewalls for several companies that were piggybacking off of the company in

Germany. By finding the common code for breaking in, they in turn gave the information over to the Americans to let them do their magic in finding all of the source codes for the money transfers made by each of the companies. The Americans and their Israeli counterparts each had other people working under them to correlate and categorize all of the information into a readable format for the decision makers to use. The teams worked together very well, especially in going after their goal of destroying a common enemy.

As each company fell under the hackers' abilities, the forensics team would begin to read the history of the business and its dealings, finding where the money went and how much of it went. At first, there were no surprises when the money flowed into Iran and Iraq and to the terrorist groups located in their countries, this was expected. It was when the money went back to Europe, into the other companies, that was the most surprising find of all. The companies that were being fed money from the terrorist countries were some that you'd least expect.

These companies were identified as mom-and-pop companies that were involved in making the parts and, in some cases, complete weapon systems used by the terrorists and other third-world countries in South America and Africa. This new information was shared, of course, with the CIA and NSA in order to find out more information about the countries and their terrorist groups. In the main room of the two computer teams there was a map hanging on the wall, which showed where the companies were located, and strings indicating what part of the world they supplied with their weapons and technology. Having this information made it possible to track the activities of the third-world countries via their own computer systems as well. It was like watching Pandora's box being opened and pulling out a new piece of the puzzle to work on every time someone reached into the box. It would take weeks for all of the information to be cataloged and documented for use. As the pieces became clearer, the need for more people became apparent. Each one of the companies that were being investigated, as well as the terrorist groups, were now needing at least two people to sift through the information. As the two original teams broke through the firewalls and started looking into their transactions and the people and countries they were dealing with, more computer specialists were added.

The information already derived from the first few companies and countries was a bonanza, considering the knowledge they gained from the way the countries did business with their friends and associates. Finding other players worldwide was a boon as to how deep the terrorists had penetrated into the governments of other countries by placing people in key places. Feeding their information to the terrorist groups meant they had an upper hand in taking down the governments they operated within. It would take teams of people and various professionals to find these people out and destroy their hold on the governments and the people they were over. With this new information, it became imperative to start the mission in order to take down the threats posed.

After the magnitude of the information was being digested, the Israeli Prime Minister called President Vance for a special meeting between the two of them in order to tackle the problem. The meeting was to take place in a neutral location, where all of the directors could be together without creating a spectacle for the press to see. It was decided they would meet in Iceland, on the base near Reykjavik, as was done during the cold war when Reagan was President of the United States. The Israeli Prime Minister decided that this would be the easiest point to get to without the press knowing what was going on.

When President Vance met with the Prime Minister, they shook hands and sat down next to each other, which was unusual. The directors each had their messengers in place to see to the needs of each country as the meeting proceeded. Each director had a copy of what was to be discussed by the leaders of the two countries. The Israelis had brought their own intelligence staff for this meeting, with the leaders of the two teams of computer geeks being present as well.

The Israeli computer hackers started off the meeting, explaining how they were able to break into the secure firewalls around each company. David said, "It was easy, once we figured the first company's computers out. The others were easy after that because the coding was the same for all of them."

The next speaker was Robert from the forensic team, who spoke of how they were able to trace all of the transactions from the beginning, and as they did so, more players began to appear in the game. With this portion of the briefing done, the next step was to look at all of the material gained from the hacking and what to do about it. At this point the room where the meeting was being held went dark and a picture from a projector, mounted on the ceiling, showed a map of the world on a screen that had been lowered from the ceiling. On the world map were places marked with red stars, indicating where the terrorist organizations had infiltrated into the countries' governments. There were red stars in both the United States and Israel, and that was a shock to the Prime Minister and his Intel staff. After the initial shock was over, the Prime Minister and the President said they both needed to fix their countries.

During the first break of the morning the President sent for the CIA and FBI directors, requesting a meeting. When they arrived, the President looked at the directors. "You know why you're here, now get to it."

"Yes, Mr. President. It will be taken care of."

The two directors walked away together, conversing with each other. "This falls under the purview of the FBI but, at this point, I think it doesn't really matter to the President," the FBI director stated.

"I agree. Let's say we work on this one together. I have a team already in place waiting to go. They can take care of the ones outside the U.S." The CIA director continued, "I expect that this will be your show?"

"Yes, let's wait and see if there is anything else the President needs us to do first. In the meantime, I'll contact my people to get them ready."

"I agree. I'll do the same as well."

At this point phone calls were made. The FBI and CIA got the ball rolling to start going after the terrorists inside and outside the United States. Internal security for the United States fell under the FBI. The FBI director called upon Sam Hatfield and his people to head the team in finding the terrorists inside America. Sam was given information and extra agents to assist in this new operation.

The rest of the meeting was devoted to identifying the locations and the terrorists that were already in place in other countries. The CIA would take part in getting rid of the terrorists, along with Israel doing their part as well. It was decided that the two countries would work together to get rid of the threats. The CIA, once more, picked Dan and John to work with Israel and their people. By the time the meeting was over, both leaders were well aware of what lay in store for them and what they must do to survive. Kill or be killed was the end result of the meeting when it came to the terrorists. And with the might of both countries, they began the next step of the operation of getting rid of the terrorists' deep state, without causing a scene for the rest of the world to see.

When the word came down to John and Dan, they halfway suspected that they would be involved in cleaning up whatever mess there was to clean up. For John, it was a matter of planning for him and the old woman, who now was his responsibility to take care of. Living in the Middle East was second nature to him and taking care of only himself was the normal flow of things. Adding the responsibility of taking care of the old woman was no real issue, except when it came to going on these types of missions, where she would be alone for who knows how long. He wasn't worried about her. He knew she could take care of herself with no problems. His concern was whether she would be okay until he got back to see to her needs in this foreign place. John and the old woman had formed an attachment to each other, like a son taking care of his mother. She in turn showed her appreciation by taking care of John in the only way she knew. That was by feeding him and taking care of his needs by keeping the bachelor pad clean for him.

They both appreciated each other and for them it was like a mother-and-son relationship, which John had never had when growing up. Being an orphan and being on his own was the norm for John, but now it was different. The two had each other and they took care of each other in the process of all they were doing. They loved each other for what they could do for each other and for what they received from each other as well.

John and Dan received word that they would be working with the Israelis, going after the terrorists that had been identified by the CIA and Israel. Their first mission was to

Ethiopia to find a well-placed man in their government who had the leader's ear. In fact, his name was Amir and he was an advisor to the Prime Minister of Ethiopia on foreign issues dealing with their country. Their job was to take him out before he could do worse damage that he was planning to do.

When Dan and John were placed with the Israeli team, they met them in Addis Ababa, Ethiopia, flying in from Riyadh, Saudi Arabia, as workers. They met in Ramada Addis, near the airport. Checking into their rooms first was the easy part of the trip so far, and meeting for dinner later that evening went without a hitch as well. Meeting their counterparts at dinner, they recognized the two Israelis, Ben Carson and David Riddle, as they had worked with them before in Iraq. Already knowing their counterparts made the job easier, in that they knew each other's capabilities.

Now it was about finding their target. Both teams had their own intel that had been hastily gathered together on Amir and were well aware of his daily routine. As they sat and ate dinner, the team discussed the target, identified as being a middle-aged man with no political ties that could be found. His name was Amir Saude, he had a wife and kids living in the city with him in their own house. He had a daily ritual of getting his coffee from the same place every day at nine o'clock, near where he worked. He would get the coffee and walk from there to his office. The first thing he would do was check his e-mail traffic from the night before and answer the most important ones first. Once that was done he would meet with the prime minister and his cabinet to discuss the current issues that were plaguing their country. When the meetings were over, it would be time for lunch and he would go out and eat at a local café and then return to finish off the e-mails that were still pending in his inbox. This daily ritual was all he did for his job. The team realized that there was no chance of him being taken out at work. This would require finding a way at night to terminate him. At this, the four men decided to watch for his after-office activities to see if anything would open up for them to take action on. Starting that night, Dan and David would work together watching Amir for the first part of the evening. Then the other team would relieve them at midnight and continue watching Amir. They then would break off for the day to sleep, only to do it again the following night.

This went on for several nights before they finally got a break from watching him. One night about ten o'clock, he left his house by himself and walked down the street and he was picked up by a car at the corner. As the car took off heading to the outskirts of the city, Dan and his cohort followed in their own car. Staying far enough back so as not to attract attention, and in the other lane, they followed the car till it reached a small house in the country. Stopping at the house, Saude got out, along with the driver, and walked into the house. Parking a little way off, Dan and David slowly crept over to the house and, seeing no guards out front, they peered into the house through the windows and saw that there was a meeting going on inside with Amir. Dan, having a small camera, took pictures of Amir who appeared to be handing something over to the man at the table. The man seated at the table thanked him and handed him some money for which Amir thanked him by shaking his hand. They talked about the next time they would meet and what the man at the table wanted from Amir. Amir stood there shaking his head no. "It will be impossible to get that kind of information so soon after delivering this information. They would think someone was stealing it for their own use."

The man at the table thought about this for a moment, "When can you bring it without any problems arising?"

"There is a possibility in about two weeks, once I report that someone has taken this information to sell it themselves."

The man at the table nodded his head, "That will be fine. Until then, my friend."

Amir left the house, riding back in the car to the street corner where he had been picked up. Dan and David followed Amir back to his residence. By now John and Ben were waiting for them to appear. Passing the new information on to the other two, for the first time they started to smile, realizing that they could now put their plan into motion, finally having something they could use to get Amir out of the way.

As Ben and John took over, David and Dan called in to their respective handlers to let them know that they finally had something to work with on Amir.

For the next two weeks, all was quiet for Amir and the two teams watching him. Then, once again, Amir walked out of his house at ten o'clock and made his way to the corner where he waited for the car. Driving back to the house just like before, Amir and the driver got out and made their way inside. This time Ben and John were already there, waiting to see what would occur. They had set up some listening equipment to eavesdrop on the conversation inside the house, which was recording as they talked.

David and Dan went up to the window and were watching everything as the tradeoff happened, again information for money. This time Dan videotaped the transaction that went on inside the house.

David went over to the car that Amir had arrived in and, using his knife, cut one of the tires, thus flattening it. After doing so, David made his way back to where Dan was videotaping the meeting. In about ten minutes the meeting was over, with Amir walking out with the driver. He was the first to notice that the tire was flat and pointed it out to the driver, who then started to change it while Amir went back into the house to wait. As the driver opened the trunk of the car to pull out the spare tire, Dan, who had quietly made his way over to where the driver was, grabbed him from behind and twisted his neck until it snapped, killing him instantly. Dragging the body over toward the house, they waited for Amir to come out to check on the driver's progress with changing the flat tire.

By now Ben and John had opened the back door to the house, sneaking in through the kitchen they made their way to the front room, and then waited in the hallway. When Amir came back in from checking on the flat tire, he mentioned to the man at the table that he couldn't find the driver anywhere. The man at the table got up and started heading towards the front door and as he did so Ben shot him in the back of the head. The man dropped in midstride to the floor. His two bodyguards were the next to be taken out by John. As they lay next to the man they had worked for, Amir seeing what happened got scared and was running out the front door. David tackled him on the front lawn and gave him a tranquilizer shot to knock him out. The team then took him to the Prime Minister's house, along with the tapes, photos, and the other information that he had on him. Dan and David carried him up to the doorstep with a note attached to him that read, "He is a traitor. Please watch the video."

Then, knocking on the door of the Prime Minister's house they left Amir bound and gagged on the front doorstep. Having completed their mission, the two teams left and returned to their apartment.

The next day there was a lot of noise coming from within the city and the Prime Minister's house about catching a spy who had been selling secrets to another group of people unheard of. It would be a week or two before they found the bodies of the man Amir had been working with and his bodyguards. After a quick trial, Amir was found guilty of treason and was put to death by a firing squad, along with his family the following week. Their bodies were left in front of their house as an object lesson for the rest of the people to see as a reminder.

As Ben and Dave were waiting to get on the plane to leave Riyadh, they saw Dan and John at the departure gate. Not showing any signs of recognition, they left, going their separate ways back to their homeland. In a few weeks they would meet again for their next target and continue their mission to destroy the terrorists' deep state. Until then, all was good.

Chapter XXII

Sam and his team were sitting in a bar where the music was loud and bad. And according to Sam, if anybody was listening to their conversation they would've been deaf by the time the meeting was over. Sam and some of his agents had followed one of their targets from a dinner with some politicians that were all about allowing illegals into the country without vetting them first. The man they had been following had plenty of money to buy their allegiance to allow this to happen. The politicians, in all of their splendor, were nothing more than a bunch of greedy dogs waiting for the big bones to be thrown out to feast on. The man who gave them the bones knew their weaknesses in women, child porn, and, of course, money.

Their target's name was Jim Hoover. He was an immigrant who had come to America years ago and was on the payroll of the government as an IT person working for the Veterans Administration (VA). Jim always had money to spare, enough to invite the right people to the right parties all over Washington, D.C. And what he couldn't buy he blackmailed with sophisticated equipment, then bribed them with money. Jim had converted to Islam and had become radicalized during his senior year in college at Rock University in West Virginia. Making his way to Europe, he then travelled to the Middle East to attend a training camp in Iran. Coming home the same way, the DHS and the FBI had no idea he was a radical Muslim. Working his way through the network and a few sympathetic power people, he was able to get a job working for the government.

He hated the American way of living, mainly because he had been raised poor by his alcoholic dad and a mother that was never there emotionally for him. He hated watching the other kids with a normal family getting what they wanted, doing the things he couldn't afford, driving cars and having friends. It wasn't until college and working twenty hours a week that he was able to buy a car. He didn't date much, between school and working part time he wasn't able to even have a girlfriend. The ones in his class wouldn't even pay attention to him because of the way he dressed. He had been an outsider in high school and it followed him into college.

One evening while working at his job as a dishwasher, he overheard some kids talking about a new religion. Eavesdropping a little to learn more about it, one of the students in the group noticed him standing there listening to them. A beautiful blond student looked at him, "Are you interested in what we were talking about?"

He didn't know what to say at first, waiting for her to tell him go to hell, but instead she asked if he wanted to join them.

Nodding his head to be closer to the blonde, they invited him into the conversation and from there he found his place at college. He attended all of the meetings they had, when he could, and participated in their activities as well. The blonde took an interest in him, which for him made it worthwhile being there. Their first date away from the group was rather awkward at first, but with the blonde's help, he was able to overcome his shyness and for the first time he was having fun in his life. Of course, he fell in love with her and it was only a matter of time that she transformed him from a poorly dressed student to a decent-looking young man. He learned from her about being clean-shaven, working, and studying to get good grades in school. Anything she suggested he did with full enthusiasm, always getting her approval when he was successful. Then came the real test, meeting some of the other Muslims in a group from another school. She introduced Jim to the other group of students, and they started asking him questions about his feelings about the religion of Islam. "Being part of this group makes me feel like I am accepted for the first time and that I have a purpose in my life. Thank you for giving it to me," he said.

They smiled at this and asked him to leave the room with the blonde. As they waited in the hallway outside the room, the blonde held his hand. "You did wonderful in there."

Smiling at her remark, he hugged her and held her until the one of the students inside the room called him back in. This time the blonde was to stay out. Walking in by himself, Jim felt all alone and wasn't sure what to think. The leader of the group looked at him and smiled, "Jim, we believe you are ready for the next step of your learning and would like you to travel with us to Europe for a couple of weeks during the summer. Would you like to do that?"

Jim didn't know what to say, except, "Can my girlfriend go with me as well?"

"No, not this time, but she will be waiting for you when you return from Europe."

Jim didn't know whether to be excited or feel bad that his blond girlfriend couldn't go with him to Europe. As he was thinking of this, the group leader said, "It was she who recommended that you should go with us."

Hearing this, Jim nodded his head, "Yes, I would like to go."

After the meeting was over, Jim stepped out into the hallway where the blonde was still there waiting for him. She rushed over to him. "Well, did they ask you to go to Europe with them?"

Jim nodded yes. "They said you recommended that I should go."

At that point, she clapped her hands and grabbed him by the arm. "Yes, I did, and you'll have lots of fun over there learning more about what we believe and what to do when it comes time."

Jim halfway smiled at her, not sure what to think about all of this, but seeing her happy made him happy. At this point she kissed him for the first time and it lingered in Jim's mind for what seemed like years. He had never been kissed by a girl before and it was really surprising to him that she did it. She grabbed him, "Come on, let's go celebrate your trip to Europe tonight, my treat."

With that, they spent the whole evening celebrating and having a good time. By the next morning Jim was completely exhausted by the night's activities and wanted to go to bed to sleep, but that would have to wait, leastwise until he got through his classes. Dragging himself home in the afternoon, after school was done, he crawled into bed and slept till the next morning.

When it came time to go to Europe, the same group of kids that interviewed him was waiting for him at the airport. Giving him his ticket and special instructions, they told him, "Someone will be there to meet you once you have landed. They will take care of you and all your needs."

When he landed in Germany he was met by another student, who showed him around all of Europe and the different places there were to see.

About the second week of his trip, Jim was invited to go to Iran for special training and to learn more about his new religion and how to use it to get what he wanted from the

Americans. There he learned about exercise, the use of weapons, RPGs, and defensive tactics to use if caught by the police. The training was hard, but Jim became pretty good at doing what he learned from the instructors. All the while they kept feeding him the concept that the Muslim religion was the only correct religion in the world and that Christians were considered infidels, to be hated and destroyed.

When he returned to America to finish school, the blonde was there to meet him at the airport and take him back to his apartment. She could tell Jim had changed while being in Europe and that he had a sense of dislike toward her because she was not his kind anymore. She was an infidel in Jim's eyes and nothing more to him.

After getting settled in his apartment again, the blond-haired woman came by to see if he needed anything. Not saying anything, he closed the door on her and went about his business in his room. Surprised by his actions, she walked away, not knowing what to think.

This had been a test for him to see if there were any feelings for the blond-haired woman anymore. Upon hearing of his reaction to the blond-haired woman, the leader of the group decided that Jim was ready for more training. The leader made it so that Jim's college was paid for and that he would only need to concentrate on being in school and being ready for the next phase of his training, which would be total mind control over the world. Jim was an excellent student, he had learned discipline from his training in Iran and it started to show in his school studies. Now he was learning what his new master expected from him and by the end of his senior year, he was ready for his new calling. With the financial backing from the group, he was able to move about like they wanted him to do. Now looking the part and acting the part as well for his new friends, he was able to get a job working for the

VA as a computer programmer. He started moving around the bar scene at night, looking for new people to get in touch with. Jim always was the party animal, buying all of the drinks for his newfound friends and having money to blow on them, because of this he attracted a lot of people to him. And in turn they introduced him to their friends, and these were the ones Jim wanted to meet.

Now being part of the in crowd, Jim was the one the people and his friends wanted to be around. Having the money and the time, he was living the dream that had escaped him for so long when he was in high school and the first part of college. Having the freedom to be and do attracted all the right people from all over, and with him paying for everything, he was able to move around in places he never knew existed.

Chapter XXIII

Sam and his team had taken turns watching Jim, now that he had been identified as a terrorist from the list that had been created by the teams that had been working together. He was one of a few that had been identified working in the United States. They had three teams watching him around the clock. Using cameras and videotape to track him became the standard for Jim, simply because of his contact with highly placed individuals in the government. Sam also knew that Jim needed to be taken out soon. His portfolio was extensive for all the wrong reasons. He was wielding a big stick over quite a few prominent people in the beltway loop. By now they had been able to download all of the information he had on the others in his group, as well as the people he was trying to blackmail. Sam was impressed with what he had seen on the downloaded material and who was affected by it. He had found enough information to go after the people on the computer to start other investigations to shut them down. However, first things first, Jim was the target for now, the others in his collection would come in due time.

Waiting to pick up Jim at the right moment was all that Sam was waiting for. Jim's itinerary never found him alone during the day, and at night he was busy playing in the different places where the beltway-loop players were. The only way for this to work was for someone to go undercover and become part of the scene themselves. After sitting and thinking about it, Sam had decided to let Bill and Jennifer play the parts in order to get next to Jim. Both were eager to play and were willing to go undercover for this operation.

Sam called in both team leads and had them sit down. He stood up and asked, "How's it going, have you found any more information about Jim?"

Both looked at each other then back at Sam, not sure what to say that hadn't already been covered in the earlier brief. "Nothing new to report at this time," Bill said, with Jennifer nodding her head in agreement.

"That's good. The reason I called you two in here is that I was thinking we needed someone to make contact with Jim and set him up to be arrested. Do you have any idea who would be good at this?"

Both Bill and Jennifer looked at each other, not saying a word. Sam continued, "I was thinking of a couple of agents posing as a couple of kids that worked the beltway as junior lobbyists. Do you have any idea of anybody that would be willing to do this?"

Bill and Jennifer again looked at each other and at the same time said, "I'll do it."

Sam smiled. "That's what I thought too."

Bill and Jennifer looked at each other, feeling slightly embarrassed that they had been set up by Sam, knowing he had already decided to pick them for it. Sam went on to say, "We'll be watching you two while you're under cover, but what we need to find out is who else is involved with this group that Jim is working for, and how big it is. We need you to confirm the information we already have and see if there's anyone else that we're not aware of."

"Yes sir, it shouldn't take too long to figure it out, sir," Bill said.

"Don't be too sure of yourself about this. This may be bigger than you think."

"Yes sir."

"I need you two to be dating, you are new to the scene, and you both are looking to have a good time while you're here. Can you do that?"

They both answered, "Yes, when do we start?"

"Tonight will be as good as any time to start. I want you to get your team together and coordinate with them so that everybody on the team knows their responsibilities and has your back while you're undercover."

"Yes sir, we will use the existing teams for coverage and add one more onto it," Jennifer said.

"Good idea. Make sure you guys have a duress signal for your team, in case things go south for you while you're under cover. Brief me before you leave for tonight."

"We'll do that, sir. Thank you for asking us to do it."

"Don't thank me until it's over and done with. Do you copy me?"

"Yes sir," they said as they hurriedly left the office to get ready.

Later that night Bill and Jennifer went back into Sam's office and laid out the plan for their coverage, who would be doing what and where they would be going. Both of them knew that Jim liked the bar scene and would go from bar to bar looking for anybody that was a possible target. The problem was they had no cover to attract Jim to them. As Sam thought about this, he asked, "Is there anybody that would vouch for either of you as being close to important people on the hill?"

Jennifer was the first to answer this question. "One of my girlfriends' dad works for a congressman from Maryland, and we used to go to her house on the weekends while at school."

"How well does he know you?"

"I'm like one of the kids there at the house."

"Will he cover for you when needed?"

"I will need to brief him, but I think he should be glad to do it for me."

"Not all of it, but enough to let him know it's important for him and you."

"Yes sir, I'll do that."

"Maybe he would be willing to go out with you tonight to celebrate your birthday by having your girlfriend and him along for the night, kind of like a double date with a chaperone to watch over both of you."

"How about we just have me and my girlfriend go out with her dad tonight just to get things started?"

"Good idea. You can meet Bill at one of the bars and maybe he can tag along for a little bit with you."

"Yes, sir, that will work. I'll call my friend right now and schedule it for tonight."

"Very good, Bill, you are her overseer for tonight. Don't let her out of your sight."

"Yes sir, I won't let her out of my sight at all."

"Now don't stalk her, you hear me?" Sam said, smiling.

Bill and Jennifer, both turning red in the face, chuckled a little. "Yes sir."

Jennifer called her friend, "Could I see you early tonight?"

Her friend, Sally, was surprised to hear from her. "Where have you been for so long? I thought you fell off the earth."

"I've been busy as of late and I was wondering if I could get with you tonight, if possible, at your house."

"Sure, why not. My parents would love to see you again too. How about dinner tonight, just like we used to do?"

"That will be fine, let's say seven o'clock?"

"Great, I'll see you then. We have so much to catch up on."

At seven o'clock Jennifer showed up and knocked on the door. Sally met her and, after hugging her, Sally took her in to see the rest of the family. It was like old home week for everybody there, and they all wanted to know what was going on in Jennifer's life since the last time she had been at the house. She said that she had become an FBI agent working in Washington, D.C., and was just newly assigned there for the white-collar crime unit. Sally's dad said to everybody sitting at the table, "Be careful what you say about my job, I could go to jail!"

Everybody laughed and, looking at Sally's dad, couldn't believe he had said that. He, of course, turned red after saying it. Jennifer knew Sally's dad to be an honest man who wouldn't do anything to put his family at risk. After the dishes were done and put away and things had quieted down, Jennifer was pulled aside by Sally. "Come on, let's go outside and sit in the porch swing."

Going out onto the porch and sitting down in the swing, Sally said, "So tell me, what's been happening since we last saw each other? Have you a boyfriend or maybe kids now?"

"Nothing new to speak much about, pretty much all quiet for me. How about you? Have you a boyfriend or maybe kids as well?"

"No, I'm still footloose and fancy free for now, although there was this one guy I really liked, but as luck would have it, he was still living at home."

"Ewww, that's not good. What happened?"

"I found out he wanted a housemaid to help raise his brothers and sisters, all ten of them."

"I bet you ran from that as fast as you could."

"Yes, I did. It wouldn't have been bad if he hadn't tried to tackle me in the front yard," Sally said, laughing. "I stiff-armed when he tried that and got away."

Jennifer knew that she needed to tell Sally the reason she had shown up after having been gone for so long. "I've sure enjoyed being back here again, seeing you and your family, and your mom is still a good cook," she said.

"Thanks, I'll tell her that. So why are you here all of a sudden?"

"Well, first off, it has been some time and I should have done this sooner than now, but the reason I'm here is that I'm going undercover after someone that is considered a terrorist and a real threat against our country."

"Yes, and?"

"And I need your help to nail him."

Sally's eyes got big and she didn't say a thing, except, "Please continue."

"I really can't say anything more than what I have already said, except to ask if you will help me."

"What do you want me to do?"

"Well, I need to talk to your dad as well before I go any further."

Sally stood up from the swing and pulled Jennifer up. "Let's go find him."

They both left the porch and headed back into the house to find Sally's dad. Finding him inside the den reading a book, Sally went over to him, "Hey, dad, can Jennifer talk to you for a minute?"

Sally's dad put his book down. "Sure, what's up?"

Jennifer related to Sally's dad everything that she had told Sally earlier and, after a minute of thinking, Sally's dad asked, "How does this concern me?"

"Well," Jennifer started out slowly, "I need to borrow your connection to the Maryland congressman that you work for, and I need to have Sally go with me to try to find this guy so that we can arrest him."

"In what way do you need my connection to the congressman?"

"You're well known and so is the congressman, and if I were a terrorist and I thought I could influence you, I would have to give it a try."

"You mean I would be the bait to nail this guy?"

"Yes, you would be the bait," as she nodded her head yes.

"How does this affect Sally here?"

"The idea I had was to go out and party like it was my birthday tonight, and we would be in the same bar as our target and, hopefully, recognizing you, he would make an attempt to come over and be part of the gang celebrating my birthday."

Sally, looking at her dad as he looked at her, shook her head yes, and her dad asked, "When is this supposed to happen?"

"Tonight, if possible, if it works for you."

Sally's dad set his book down. "Let's do it. Give me a minute to change clothes."

Jennifer let out a sigh of relief after Sally's dad agreed to do it. "Let me call my backup and let him know we are on our way out."

Sally's dad went upstairs to change and Sally jumped up and down, thinking how much fun it would be following a bad guy around for a while tonight. Jennifer said to Sally, "I need you to remember that this is about catching him to find out more about him, so don't overplay your hand tonight."

Sally nodded her head, smiling. "I wonder if this is how James Bond does it?"

As the three of them drove down into the bar section of town, they stopped at the different bars that Jim was supposed to frequent on a nightly basis. Jennifer and Sally were quite loud as they celebrated Jennifer's birthday and stayed until Bill told Jennifer that Jim was at another bar down the street. Getting into the dad's car they drove over to the bar and went in, with Jennifer yelling, "Bartender, I want a round of drinks for my friends here. It's my birthday today!"

The bartender nodded and had one of the waitresses come over with the drinks. As the waitress was setting the drinks down on the table, both Sally and Jennifer were giggling and laughing at the guys that were in the bar. Jim, who was standing at the bar, heard all the noise and couldn't help but notice that both girls were feeling their oats as they sat there drinking their beers. Jim recognized the old man with the two girls from newspaper photos he had seen, and he knew he was important. Jim, taking a chance, bought another round of drinks for the girls, assuming the old man was the designated driver for the evening. Bill, who had slipped in earlier, was watching Jim as he sent the round of drinks over to the girls, who were still laughing and carrying on. After a minute or two the drinks Jim had ordered appeared at the girls' table and, looking around to see who had sent them, Jennifer yelled out, "Thank you to our knight in shining armor!"

That was Jim's cue to wander over to the table. Bill had already contacted Jennifer through her earwig that Jim was on his way over. Jennifer nodded and waited. Jim made a grand entrance coming over to the table where the girls sat drinking their drinks. He showed up saying, "I hear it's your birthday today and I thought I would help you celebrate it."

"Are you the one that bought these drinks for us?" Jennifer asked.

"Guilty as charged."

"Well, in that case, sit down and join us since these drinks are yours," Jennifer said with a smile.

"You know, he's kind of cute," Sally said.

Sally's dad sat there not saying a word about his daughter's remark. Jim looked at the old man sitting there and asked,

"Aren't you the guy that works with the congressman from Maryland?"

"As a matter of fact, I am, and this is his daughter, Jennifer. I promised the old man I would keep an eye on the girls tonight so they wouldn't get into any trouble," Sally's dad said.

"That's good of you to take care of his daughter like this."

"It's the least I can do for him since he is my boss and all. What is it that you do for a living?"

"Please forgive me, my name is Jim and I work for the VA as one of their computer geeks, as they say."

"So, you take care of our boys when they come home all shot up from the war?"

"Yes, I do, and I want you to know it has been a real pleasure being there to help them after everything they have been through."

"I bet the congressman would like to meet you and thank you for all you do to assist these soldiers in their recovery," Sally's dad said.

"It would be my honor to do so."

"How about tonight, since I have to watch over his daughter and bring her home."

"That would be fine, if it's not inconvenient to do so," Jim said, as he thought to himself, *"Here's the chance I've been waiting for, somebody important, not just a lackey."*

"Then it's settled, one more round and we'll take the girls home. Then you can meet the congressman."

The girls feigned not liking it when Sally's dad said it was time to go home, putting up a fight just for a little bit. But Sally's dad said, "You guys have jobs to go to tomorrow and you don't want to be so hung over that you can't work."

Jennifer was the most outspoken. "If we sneak in real quiet, maybe my dad won't hear us."

So off they went, all four of them heading out the door of the bar and into the car Sally's dad was driving. Bill, watching all of this, got into his own car and drove to the congressman's house and waited for them to arrive, with two other agents following behind Jennifer's car. Jim was excited about meeting the congressman from Maryland and was asking all sorts of questions about the man and what kind of person the congressman was. Sally's dad answered all of his questions with patience and, after driving for twenty minutes, pulled in front of the congressman's house.

Jim, helping the girls get out of the car, walked up to the front door of the house. Getting ready to ring the doorbell, Jennifer slipped away from Jim and started running, and as she did so she fell to the ground laughing. Jim went after her and, leaning over to pick her up, Jennifer grabbed his wrist and pulled him down to the ground. By now Bill was there as well and helped pin Jim to the ground. Not knowing what was going on, Jim struggled to get up but, because of Bill's weight, Jim was held in place. Cuffing him and then picking him up, Bill identified himself as an FBI agent and advised Jim he was under arrest for being a terrorist. By now the other two agents were leading Jim back to their car. Jennifer got up and walked over to Sally and her dad. "Thank you for helping us in this."

"Think nothing of it. Just so you know, he has been hanging out in the same offices I work at lately, trying to get to know people where I work," Sally's dad said.

"That's good to know. We may need to talk to you more later, once we get him squared away."

"Anytime."

Jennifer looked at Sally, "You really think he's cute?"

"I did that for my dad, to see if I could rattle him," Sally replied, laughing.

"You're grounded until you're eighty years old, do you hear me, young lady?" Sally's dad looked at her as he too laughed.

"I guess we'll see you again sometime, when you need us to save the world, huh?"

"I promise it won't be that long again; besides, I get to tell you what happens to this guy, seeing as how you're involved with his apprehension."

By now Bill was coming up to where Jennifer was standing talking to Sally. "We need to go now."

Sally, looking at Bill, said, "Well, well, well, no wonder you joined the FBI. Where do I sign up?"

Jennifer and Bill's faces turned red and they laughed as they walked away. Sally's dad yelled out, "She gets that from her mom's side of the family."

As Jennifer got into the car, Bill reached over, hugging her. "Well, that went well."

"Are you kidding? I've never been so scared in my life."

"Well, you couldn't tell it from where I was watching."

"How about some food before we go back to the office to interrogate our terrorist?"

Jennifer looked at Bill. "I'm glad you were my backup on this, I knew I could count on you." Reaching over, she kissed him on the cheek.

Bill was speechless and grabbed her hand and wouldn't let it go for the rest of the evening. Jennifer was in seventh heaven knowing Bill felt the same way as she did.

Getting back from their dinner break, Bill went in with Jennifer and reported to Sam about how they caught Jim and that they wanted to go in and interrogate him on what he knew. "Not to worry, I'll be doing the interrogation tomorrow morning. You both need to go home for the night.

Good job, both of you," Sam said, pleased with his new agents.

The two agents, looking at their boss and then at each other, smiled as they walked out of his office.

Chapter XXIV

The third Israeli team was sent to Somalia to destroy the terrorist camp and the people in it. Having copied the U.S. Navy Seal transport system, the semi-autonomous mini submarine (SAMS). The six-man team was delivered by an Israeli submarine off the coast of Somalia. Leaving the SAMS, they swam to shore. Stowing all their diving equipment that wasn't needed in a sand pit to be picked up after their mission was complete. They then made their way to the new compound, where the terrorists had set up operations once again after their first compound was blown up and destroyed, losing half of their force.

With only a week to find the new camp and using satellite photos supplied by the U.S., the team scoured the area and found the new compound on the second day. The team was about ready to leave when they stumbled upon it by accident. Sitting on a ridge, watching the traffic on the road below, one of the spotters noticed that some of the trucks had wood and tools inside the beds. Taking a chance, they followed the trucks about five miles up the road. Staying on the ridge line, they saw the compound being rebuilt by a small band of workers, who were being guarded by other men with weapons. As the team watched the building, they noticed that the they were digging holes with heavy equipment and that the holes were at least ten feet down.

Letting their handlers know the location of the new camp, the team sat and watched the building of the compound go on for another week. By the end of the week the holes they had been digging had taken shape and now the walls were in place. From all guesses, it was to be a below-ground bunker for weapons storage. As the final touches were being put on the bunker walls, the terrorists started loading their weapons into the bunker.

This was what the Israeli team was waiting for. With the weapons in the bunker they could be destroyed all at once. After a couple of more days the bunker was completed with all the weapons inside. Now it was up to the Israelis to do their part. Waiting until it was night, they quickly moved through the compound. Taking out each of the guards one by one, the team brought their bodies to the bunker. After laying them inside the bunker, they set charges to go off as soon as the terrorists would be there to start work the following morning. They quickly made their way back up to the ridge, there they waited for the terrorists to show up.

At about six o'clock the following morning, the workers and the terrorists showed up to start work. As the workers got their tools and equipment ready, one of the foremen noticed that the night guards were missing, a search was organized to look for the guards. Eventually, one of the workers found their bodies inside the bunker. As the terrorists gathered around to see what had happened, the Israelis, who were watching from the ridge, flipped the switches on the detonators, thereby triggering the blasting caps and detonating the bombs inside the bunker. The explosion was felt all the way up to the ridge, and the shockwave came a few seconds later. When the smoke and dust had finally settled, there was a great big hole in the ground with nobody around it. All the terrorists were evaporated by the heat of the blast from the explosion, and the workers bodies were just bits and pieces and barely recognizable as human remains.

The next day the Israelis were waiting for their ride back to Israel via the submarine. As they waited, the Somali government was on high alert, looking for whoever had destroyed the terrorists and their camp. Thinking that it was Ethiopia, they started building an army to destroy their terrorist training camps inside their country. By the time they were done, two more terrorist camps were destroyed by the Somali government forces. The Ethiopian army was massing themselves for war against Somalia in return for their crossing the border into their territory. Israel didn't say a word, hoping that the two countries would find more terrorist camps and do their work for them. It would be another six weeks before the war between them would finally come to an end.

When done, the three teams were back in Israel and were resting before their next mission into Syria to take out the Scud missiles. The Scuds were supposed to have been removed, according to the photos taken by the drone, and from the looks of it, they had been removed, at least the ones close to the border. It wasn't until the satellite photos appeared from the U.S. that they noted anything was wrong. According to the photos, there had been some activity going on about 50 miles in from the border. Although it would take expert photo specialists to see the disturbance on the ground, the specialists could tell that something had occurred in the area. There were tracks leading to and from the place of interest, with nothing being there where the tracks stopped. This puzzled the Israeli Intel people, compelling them to send another drone into the area to have a closer look at the tracks in that part of the desert. They found on further inspection of the photos taken that there were mounds there, which meant something was buried in the desert out there.

The Israelis, not wanting to be surprised by missiles they didn't know about, decided to mount a two-prong operation into Syria. The first team would go in and verify that the Scud's closest to Israel were actually gone. The second team, who had the higher risk, would go deeper into Syria to look into the mounds in their desert.

Under cover of darkness, the two teams were inserted into Syria. The group looking at the border issue would have the easier task of verifying the removal of the missiles. The team would walk into and verify that the missiles were gone. The other team would have to be flown in under cover of radar and then dropped into the area. The second team would have the hardest time getting in and getting out without being seen by Syrian surveillance radar.

According to the tactics and capabilities of the aircraft and the team members, it was decided to travel across the desert in an Osprey tilt-wing aircraft. Flying below the radar coverage of the Syrian surveillance radar system, they would set down near the mounds in the desert to allow the team to examine them. The aircraft would stay there until the team came back, then lift off and again fly below radar coverage back into Israel. Using the Osprey aircraft would provide the easiest ingress to and egress from the target. The Osprey was the first tilt-wing aircraft to be used by the U.S. Marines for delivery of troops into combat. Still having bugs to be worked out, the aircraft was the best option to use for the Israelis. Borrowing one from the United States, they took the Osprey and, as usual, modified the aircraft to do more than the U.S. had done with it. This was a trademark capability of Israel, to take what they had been given from the United States and modify it to meet their own needs in the type of war they fought in the desert against other countries. The most awesome sight was to see the Israeli F-16 after the modifications were completed. The Israeli F-16 looked like it was on steroids.

Getting the Osprey from the U.S. Marines, with the understanding that after the modifications were done on the Osprey, the Marine Corps would be able to have a list of the modifications that were made for future use by the Department of Defense. Being able to keep the modified aircraft for combat in the desert would meet the needs of the Israeli Special Forces and would allow them greater flexibility in combat.

The team loaded into the aircraft, the plane took off and headed into the night and as it got closer to the border, the pilot, using night-vision goggles and terrain-following radar on board the aircraft, entered into Syrian airspace and went down to twenty feet, flying through the canyons and valleys, staying close to the mountains to mask their position to the Syrian radar. Within fifteen minutes, the aircraft stopped and settled down onto the desert floor. The pilots would wait for the team or leave as needed in case of emergency. The radioman listened to the chatter on the radio. Not picking up anything except the normal chatter, he signaled the pilot that everything was okay. They would sit and wait for the team to come back, having their guards posted, surrounding the aircraft.

The leader of the group led his men in the direction of the GPS coordinates. By all calculations it was five miles to the mounds, walking on a dry river bed. Moving fast and quiet, they made good time to the mounds. It was as they had seen from the photographs. After checking into the mounds, they found six of them. The team start digging into the mounds, they dug for about an hour before hitting something hard in one of the mounds. Clearing away the sand and dirt, they found the Scud missiles on their launchers, all covered in tarps. Pulling away the tarps, they found the control panel in the trailer on top of the truck. After taking pictures of the setup, they radioed the team boss, who was waiting to hear from them. After confirming the location of the Scuds, they were told to cover them back up and return to base.

Making the hike back to the Osprey, they boarded the plane and prepared for takeoff. Having the exact coordinates would make it easy to destroy the missiles where they lay buried in the sand. As the Osprey started lifting off the ground, one of the team saw some Syrian soldiers on patrol and reported it to the team leader. Telling the pilots to set the Osprey back down on the ground and ordering the men back into the desert, they prepared to meet the Syrian soldiers. As the team was spread out, they waited for the Syrians to get closer. The soldiers, having heard the plane's engines, came up over the hill looking to see what it was. Moving slowly through the desert, they made their way to the Osprey. As the last soldier went past the first Israeli team member, he was jumped by the Israeli soldier and killed by stabbing him with a knife, leaving the Syrian soldier for dead. Slowly the rest of the Israeli team moved closer to the Syrian soldiers, taking them out one by one until they were all accounted for. All the Syrian soldiers were buried in the sand and left for the animals to find.

Once again, the team loaded into the Osprey and this time left to go back to Israel to report what they had found. Upon landing, the photos taken were immediately developed and sent to the Intel Chief for review. He then verified that they were Scud missiles and took the pictures to the Senior Intel Chief who in turn took them to the Prime Minister.

The first team did find remains of a Scud missile setup, but nothing showed that they were still there. Again taking pictures to verify no missiles were in place, the team headed back to its own border.

As the Prime Minister looked over the pictures, he asked the Senior Intel Chief his opinion on what to do. He said, "Of course, we will destroy them, but we need to make it look like something else caused them to be destroyed."

"What do you suggest?" the Prime Minister asked.

"I don't know for sure. Let me have a little time to think it over, and I will get back to you on it."

"Very well, you have two days to come up with something."

"Yes sir," he said as he headed out the door looking for the rest of his staff to come up with a plan.

Chapter XXV

Banker Montoya was finally able to catch a break, getting out of Mexico on board a transport ship heading to the Middle East. He had paid the customs people off to get aboard the ship, and he knew he would have to pay again once reaching the docks in Mogadishu.

It wasn't where he wanted to go but still a short distance from his destination in Somalia. He was wanting to go to Somalia, but without a passport he was left to his own ways and means to get himself there. Clutching his briefcase, he knew he had the resources to get him to Somalia, in fact, in comfort.

Docking in Mogadishu and getting off the boat was easy, the captain of the ship helped him by hiding him among the supplies that were dropped off at the dock, and it only cost an extra thousand dollars to get it done. Once there, he knew he would need some transportation to move around. Finding a good used vehicle here would be hard. Being able to find a used-car lot in Mogadishu was not going to be fun. However, the hotel he was staying at had a source for securing a Land Rover for extended trips into the desert, which was one of their perks for the tourists who stayed at the hotel. Getting up the next morning with a guide to take him to Berbera, Somalia, he left Mogadishu in hopes of meeting the terrorist leader he had done business with while in Mexico.

Driving from Mogadishu to Berbera took a couple of days of traveling across dirt roads and being stopped every so often by the military. It was the bandits that posed a greater problem for the bank president. Being able to hide his money from them proved to be quite a task. Arriving on the third day and driving up to the prison where the terrorist leader would be, he opened the door of the Land Rover and walked up to the gate of the prison that was being guarded and knocked on the prison door. "Is Assad here? If so, I would like to speak to him."

The sentry at the door looked at him. "Assad is no longer here."

Montoya couldn't understand why he wasn't there. "Where can I find him?"

"He should be in the hotel, in the market center."

Thanking the sentry, Montoya left, saying to his guide, "Take me to the market center in town."

The guide drove through the city looking for the market center and, finally finding it, parked in front of the hotel. The banker got out once again and went into the hotel up to the front desk and asked for Assad.

The desk clerk, looking through the hotel register, found that Assad was in room 206, and he pointed at the stairs going up to the second floor. Knocking on the door to the room, Assad answered and seeing Montoya standing there, he reached out and hugged him. After being invited into the room, they sat down together. Montoya asked, "So why are you staying at the hotel instead of the prison?"

"Some U.S. soldiers came in and took the President and shot up everything in the process. I was lucky to get out alive. Thinking that they might try again, I decided to stay here at the hotel."

"I'm so sorry for you. I had the same thing happen to me. I barely escaped from Mexico."

"So, we two are brothers running from the same people."

"Yes, we are at that."

"What can I do to help you, now that you are here?"

"I'm looking for a place to lie low for a while, leastwise until the heat goes cold."

Assad laughed at the statement, shaking his head in agreement. "Believe me, I understand how you feel. Let me do some checking and I'll let you know what I find for you."

"That's good. I trust that they have room for me here in the hotel."

"I will make sure they do for you, my friend."

With that, Assad made all the reservations for Montoya to have a room and a place to clean up and get some new clothes to wear. Montoya sent the driver back to Mogadishu with plenty of money for his time. Finally, being able to relax and eat some good cooked food was a welcome change for Montoya. When he had been on the road, they didn't have a campfire at night and had to eat cold food to survive. This was because of the bandits roaming the countryside at night. Getting a shower and shave made a vast improvement on Montoya, making him feel like a new man. Seeing Assad was good for his soul because he knew he could trust him on anything.

After a few days Assad got back to the banker, "I have found a place to live in that should meet your needs. It's just outside the city and has all the amenities you need to be comfortable." Montoya was anxious to see the place. "When can we go see it?" he asked Assad.

"This afternoon, if that is okay for you."

"This afternoon is fine."

Assad picked up the banker at one o'clock that afternoon and they drove over to look at the place. It was as Assad had said it would be. Montoya looked it over, "This will do."

"That is good to hear, my friend."

When all of the exchanges and papers were signed, Montoya moved into the house and had Assad become his permanent house guest as well. This was done not only out of friendship but for security purposes for both of them. This way the terrorist groups and the military would leave them alone as they lived in obscurity. All of this took about thirty days to complete. For Montoya, it had turned out well, considering all that he had lost by his previous standard of living. Assad was happy to have a place to call his own and was happy to have a friend to share it with. Considering everything, all was going well.

For the next six months life was good for both of them. Assad was recruiting once again to build his terrorist organization back up to what it once was. Still having the contacts from his past, he relied heavily on them to rebuild it. Montoya was assisting in this endeavor for the sake of making money for himself and regaining his wealth as well. All seemed well as they created their networks again. In fact, Montoya was thinking of leaving and going back to Mexico to pick up where he had left off. Montoya was homesick and was ready to go back. Assad was ready get things started again as well. He now had fifty men that were under his control and ready to follow him wherever he went. In fact, the training was being held near the house in which Montoya and Assad lived. The time was right for a change for both of them now. Although they were still working together and still friends, it was time to part ways.

All the while, the CIA had been watching all of the buildup of the terrorist network going on in Berbera and saw recent military training from their real-time satellite feeds going on just outside of the city. Thinking that another terrorist group, that had been part of the kidnapping of the President, was starting up again, they decided action was needed to stop it.

Passing the information over to the Department of Defense, the U.S. Navy became interested in what was happening in Somalia again. Sending in another team of observers to verify, they confirmed that another terrorist group was training in the area, being led by the same man as before. Slipping in another team of Seals to wipe out the terrorist group was the next thing on the agenda for the Navy.

Coming in at night, using a submarine to set the team in place, the Seals moved quietly through the desert. Finding the terrorists asleep with the token guards watching over the group, the Seals quickly killed the guards, using silencers on their guns. Going from group to group and placing charges inside the buildings where the terrorists slept was done in minutes. They went into the house and found Assad and Montoya asleep. Grabbing them both, they drugged the two of them and carried them from the house to one of the rubber boats waiting for them. Once everything was complete, the Seal team returned to the submarine and waited for all the Seals to be accounted for. The leader of the team detonated the bombs that had been planted inside the sleeping areas of the terrorists. The explosions all occurred at once and the terrorists were gone in a split second. The new threat from the terrorist group was over. Running a facial scan on their captives, Assad was identified quickly and was put into a confined place as he recovered from the drugs the Seal team had given him. The face of the banker took longer to find, and after a while he was identified as a drug-cartel person of interest who was wanted in Mexico on drug charges and other assorted warrants.

When both men were awake and had recovered from the effects of the drugs, they couldn't believe their eyes that they were aboard an American submarine going to the United States. Both Assad and Montoya knew it was over for them.

Being escorted off the submarine and put in jail, it was just a matter of time for the trial and the incarceration of Assad in Florence, Colorado. Montoya was sent back to Mexico to face charges there. Being found guilty, he was sent to a Mexican prison to serve his time.

One day the police chief came to visit Montoya while he was in prison. Montoya recognized him. "What can I do for you?"

"Nothing. I'm just making sure you are here in prison and that you'll be here for a long time to come," the chief said, smiling.

Montoya looked at him. "You don't know how long I'll be in here, Chief."

"Oh, but I do. As soon as you're done here, the Americans want to extradite you to their side of the border to face charges there as well. The Americans are filing paperwork on you as we speak, to transfer you to their side of the border to stand trial for your crimes in America."

The banker didn't know this. He smiled, "At least they'll treat me better there."

"Once again you haven't heard, so I'll enlighten you. If you're found guilty in America, you will serve your sentence here in Mexico, in this prison not there. Mexico has signed an agreement with the United States, an MOU (Memo of Understanding), if you will, to have people who are not citizens of the U.S. and are convicted of crimes in the United States, serve their time in their original country. Since your network covered Mexico and the U.S., you will continue to serve your time here."

As the chief walked away, he laughed aloud, not saying a word as he walked out of the prison and left the complex to go back to his car.

The Counterfeit President

Montoya was surprised by this and didn't know what to say to the chief's remarks and slowly got up from the table and started back to his cell, knowing he would be in prison for a very long time now. Even the guard escorting him was laughing.

Chapter XXVI

As the Prime Minister sat at his desk, two days had gone by and he was waiting for the Senior Intel Chief to come for their agreed-upon meeting. The meeting would be held to discuss the steps needed to take out the Scuds that were found buried in the Syrian desert. The Prime Minister kept looking at his watch, getting a little nervous as to why the Intel Chief wasn't there already.

At two minutes prior to the agreed-upon time the secretary opened the Prime Minister's door to announce that the Intel Chief was outside waiting to talk to him. After getting seated in a chair opposite the Prime Minister, the chief said, "Sorry to keep you waiting, Prime Minister, but I was delayed due to getting some final paperwork about the Scud site."

"What have you learned since we last talked?"

"Well, basically nothing has changed, except that there is more activity going on around the missile site. It seems that the Syrians are missing one of their desert patrols from that area and have started to try to find out what happened to them."

"Is this a problem to us?"

"Not yet, but if they find the dead soldiers we could have a problem, if they find out it was us that killed them."

"Do you have any plans for me to see, about how to take care of the missiles?"

"Yes sir, first off, the team that we sent to Syria by foot found no Scuds in their area, which was the closest to the border. The second team was able to find the ones in the desert that were buried, as you have seen from the pictures.

"Yes, I reviewed them all and read their reports."

"I have two options, maybe more, for you to consider. The first one is an aircraft strike, or a UAV (unarmed aerial vehicle) drone would work as well. The second option would be sending in another team to blow them up. That being said, now that the Syrians are looking for their dead soldiers, the area could be too hot to handle."

"What do you suggest, then?"

"I think we need to keep Israel out of this, if it's possible to do so. The Syrians will think we did it, anyway, but if we mislead them by throwing them off the trail, we could pull it off."

"We could steal one of their planes, fly it into the Scuds, and pick up the pilot before they knew we were there."

The question now sitting on the table was what was the best way to get the Scuds without starting a war that would impact all of the Middle East. The Prime Minister knew he had to make a decision, and soon. The safety and peace of Israel was at stake. Thinking aloud, he said, "Who would be crazy enough to go behind enemy lines, steal a jet, and then crash it into a missile site?"

"I know of one pilot who could pull it off and probably survive as well."

"Who would be crazy enough to do that?"

"The one man that comes to mind is a major in the IAF (Israeli Air Force), who is known for his grandstanding and also for having the most kills in air-to-air combat against the bad guys."

"What's his name?"

"Major Aaron Herzog. He is crazy enough to want to do this just for bragging rights. He has two thousand hours in the F-15 and another thousand hours flying the old F-4 Phantom. He's a good pilot."

"When can I meet this major?"

"It just so happens I have him waiting outside with the secretary."

"Are you sure that it's safe for the secretary being out there alone with him?" The Prime Minister smiled as he asked the question.

"Hard to say, Prime Minister. I'll go get him."

Opening the door, the major was indeed talking to the secretary, trying to get her number for later, when the Intel Chief called to him to come in to meet the Prime Minister. After standing up and walking into the office, the Intel Chief introduced the major to the Prime Minister, who looked at the major for a second. "I hear from our colleague here that you want to try to capture a MiG-21 and crash it into a missile site."

"Yes, sir, I believe I can crash anything that flies, sir," the major replied.

The Intel Chief shook his head and closed his eyes for a second, then opened them again. The Prime Minister smiled when he saw the Intel Chief do this. "Well, I hope you're that good at flying and bringing yourself out alive as well, Major."

"I will do my best, sir."

"Has the Chief here told you what we want you to do?"

"Yes sir, steal a plane and fly it into a missile site on the Syrian side of the border. Sounds easy enough to do."

After looking at the major and thinking for a minute, the Prime Minister looked at the Intel Chief. "How long will it take to get him up to speed?"

The major interrupted, "I'm ready now, sir."

"It's just a matter of getting transportation for him to get to the air base where he will steal the airplane from. We have a team all ready to go to take him there," the Intel Chief said.

The Prime Minister looked at both of them. "You know, this just might work. Good luck, Major, and Godspeed to you."

"Yes sir."

After the two of them left the Prime Minister's office, the Intel Chief looked at him, "Do you think you can do this, Major?"

"If not, at least it will have been fun trying, sir."

"What about your date with the secretary, Major?"

"Not to worry, Chief. I'll be back for the date."

Later that night the major was dressed in camos (camouflage clothing), waiting for the rest of the team to appear. Using the Osprey once again, the team boarded, along with the major, and took off into the night, heading into Syria. Again flying below radar coverage, they made their way across the border into Syria, heading to a known airfield in the Daraa Province toward an air base called Tha'leh. The base was in Syrian control and had been involved in fighting against ISIS. Both sides had seen some intense fighting, and the once-beautiful city was now nothing more than a casualty of war.

It would take three hours of flying to get close enough for the team to insert the major onto the airbase. Once the major was inside the base, he would be on his own and the team would head back to the Osprey and exit out of Syria. Hopefully, the major would find an aircraft that would be suitable for his mission. Landing in the desert, next to the base, the major and his escort team took off for the air base. Traveling by night was dangerous at best because of the land mines that had been placed by the Syrian army to stop ISIS from trying to get on the base. These land mines encircled the base and only certain high-ranking Syrian officers knew their actual locations. The team used mine detectors, which gave them more time to find a path through the mine fields without being seen. After walking about three miles across the desert, the major got his first break from hiking to regain his strength. At this point he commented, "I'm sure glad I'm a pilot instead of being a soldier. This hiking can kill you."

His teammates looked at him, laughing, with one of them saying, "This aint nothing; we have to go back the same way we came in. You get to fly out!"

Off in the distance they could see the lights of the airbase showing in the sky. Knowing they were close, they continued moving on. Reaching the fence perimeter, the team assisted the major over the barbed wire and onto the other side. Getting his bearings and looking again at the map, he headed toward the hangars at the end of the runway. Saying goodbye, the team took off back out into the desert to get to the Osprey.

The major walked toward the aircraft parked on the flight line, where he found what he was looking for, a MiG-21, fully loaded, on alert waiting to be flown. Now he needed to find the ground crew to get it started. Looking around for the generator to start the jet engine, he found one near a second MiG-21. Heading into the flight shack, he found a flight suit inside one of the lockers. Quickly changing his clothes, he put on the flight suit and headed back out onto the flight line where the two MiGs were sitting. Calling one of the ground crew over, he had the technician start the generator and then helped connect the power cables to the MiG-21 to get it started. By now the noise of the MiG-21 starting up got everybody's attention. Climbing into the MiG-21, he told the ground-crew member to disconnect the power cables to the

MiG. After telling the ground crew that he was testing the engine and running it up to full power, the jet started taxiing down the ramp towards the runway. Being one of the alert jets, it was already positioned near the runway, and within minutes he was airborne and flying toward Israel. The second MiG-21 was still sitting there when one of the ground crew called up to find out about the engine test. Nobody had any idea of what he was talking about. Sensing something was wrong, a Syrian pilot was told to go after the first MiG-21 and, if necessary, shoot it down. Getting airborne, the second MiG-21 was in full afterburner, trying to catch up with the first MiG.

After reaching normal altitude, the major checked his weapons status, finding he had a full arsenal on board his MiG. He had air-to-air missiles, his cannons were fully loaded, and he was carrying extra fuel tanks in case he needed to go a greater distance than planned for. In fact, he had two 500-pound bombs aboard, one under each wing, as well. Racing across the sky, he loaded the coordinates of the Scud missile location into his navigation system. Flying the plane and watching his radar, an alarm went off signifying that another jet was airborne, coming from his six o'clock position. Turning off his running lights and going dark, he thought just maybe the second MiG would fly past him. As the second MiG got closer, his Radar Warning Receiver (RWR) started sounding off in his helmet. This was normal for this kind of flying, it's when you get a different tone of being locked on for a missile shot that makes the pilot nervous. Sure enough, within seconds the lock-on tone came next, requiring the major to take evasive maneuvers to break missile lock. Banking right, the major was able to break the missile lock and, turning his aircraft in a tight turn, came up on the second MiG's six o'clock position. He then flipped his pickle switch to arm his air-to-air missiles. Once he got tone, the second MiG went into a tight turn as well, trying to lose the major. Now the major's experience of fighting the MiG-21 came into play. Knowing the weakness of the aircraft better than the Syrian MiG pilots, he stayed with the second MiG, closing the gap as he chased him across the night sky. The MiG the major was flying was a beast and he needed every bit of strength to fly it. Keeping up with the second MiG was at times all he could do. It wasn't like flying the F-15 at all. Finally, catching the other MiG pilot, who was flying erratically by now, he got closer. Turning off his missiles, he used his cannons and fired at the second MiG. Seeing the tracers flying past his cockpit canopy, the pilot once again panicked and started flying wildly. This time the major turned on his missiles again. After getting good tone he fired a missile at the second MiG. The pilot of the second MiG was too scared to remember what to do, and the missile locked onto the aircraft with its radar and flew right up to the wing of the MiG, exploding and ripping the right wing off of the MiG. All the pilot could do was eject and hope somebody would find him.

Having shot down the second MiG, the Major recalibrated the coordinates on his navigation system and flew on to the Scud sight. After reaching the site, instead of crashing, he decided to drop the two 500-pound bombs onto the target. Once dropping the bombs, he got on the Syrian Air Force frequencies, yelling, "May Day! May Day!" When this was complete, he flew over the missile site to make sure the missiles had been taken out before flying down onto the deck and going below radar coverage. Having the two 500-pound bombs gone allowed him a little more maneuverability to fly closer to the ground.

Finding the right radio frequency, the major called IDF (Israel Defense Forces) radar control and asked for landing instructions. Arriving at the base with an armed escort from two F-15s, he landed the MiG and got out of the aircraft just as the Osprey was coming in to land as well. The Senior Intel Chief was there to meet him on the tarmac, shaking his hand and asking about the missile site.

"Instead of crashing the plane into the missile site, I dropped some bombs on it. Plus, I brought home a brand-new MiG-21 for Israel to play with," the major said.

The Intel Chief was ecstatic with the mission being a success, plus getting a MiG-21 to boot. As the major walked away, the Chief said, "We need to debrief you, Major."

"Not right now, I have a date with the Prime Minister's secretary," he said as he quickly got into a jeep and headed to find the secretary.

Chapter XXVII

As President Vance read the reports from the directors of the FBI, CIA, and NSA, he was pleased with what the reports told him. The FBI and CIA had been rounding up the terrorists all over the world, especially here in the United States. The NSA hadn't picked up any more chatter than usual, which meant the terrorists were not aware of what was happening to them throughout the world. Eventually, they would realize that the moles were being taken out, but until then the United States and Israel would continue moving forward against their common threat. At least for now, the world was safer and the bad guys, so to speak, were not aware of what was going on.

Sam Hatfield and his team were still going after the terrorists inside America and, with the help of his team of junior FBI agents, were nailing them. The best part about this was there was no news coming out about their work being accomplished. If and when they caught a terrorist, they were automatically sent to Gitmo, awaiting a secret trial to be sentenced for being terrorists.

Dan and John, working with Ben and David, had no rules to follow in the apprehension of the terrorists they were going after. The terrorists were turned over to the Israelis to deal with, which was usually final and complete, in that they were never heard of again. The rights of the individual terrorists were based on the intent of what they were going to do against the rights and intents of others they hated.

As the President continued reading the reports, he thought about the ex-President and the first lady sitting in prison for the rest of their lives, wondering if they had started to appreciate what they had done to themselves and what they tried to do to America. He looked up from the paperwork and looked at the directors. "Well, gentlemen, it looks as if we won this round in the game called the Middle East."

"Yes, we did. We were very lucky this time," replied the CIA director, speaking for the others as well.

President Vance acknowledged the comment, "We must be doing something right, and as long as we keep doing it, we will always come out on top."

The End

Epilogue

President Vance was re-elected for a second term as President of the United States, on the platform of keeping America safe from an unknown enemy both foreign and domestic.

Sam Hatfield was designated as the go-to person for apprehending the terrorists, and his team was given carte blanche to go after the terrorists inside the United States. The team would never be split up and they would operate like this until all of the terrorists were taken down. The team that Sam had put together was the best answer to the terrorist threat in America and would continue for the rest of their time spent in the FBI. In the end, they apprehended twenty sleeper terrorists in the United States, among others that were pro-terrorists as well. The commendations and awards received for their work were classified and would only be found in their personnel records.

Bill and Jennifer's relationship continued to grow. Keeping it on the down low, they continued working with Sam Hatfield's team until they both retired to let someone else take their places.

The team of computer geeks that were from America and Israel continued to work together in directing the actions of the CIA and Mossad against the terrorists. They would continue to do this as they dug deeper into the computer records. In their work they found another organization inside Saudi Arabia and Iraq and were able to dismantle them before they could do any damage.

The major did get his date with the Prime Minister's

secretary and bragging rights of capturing a MiG-21 for the Israelis. He would later be promoted to Lieutenant Colonel/Squadron Commander and teach the rookie pilots how to fight and fly against the MiG-21 and other MiG aircraft. He would later marry the Prime Minister's secretary and raise three boys that were just like him, karma. His wife would laugh as he saw how their sons were.

Banker Montoya would spend the rest of his life in prison, never getting out, and was eventually killed by an unknown assailant while there.

Assad was sentenced to Florence, Colorado, as a cellmate with the ex-President. They both were put into solitary confinement because of the attempts made on their lives while in prison. Seems as if traitors can't stand traitors either.

The first lady would never see her husband again while in prison and would eventually die in prison from old age for her part in killing all of the people on board Air Force One.

The ex-President's children would never recover from the fact that their parents were traitors to America and ended up moving to another country to get away from the harassment of being children of the traitor President.

Alvarez, the electronics man from Mexico, stayed in the United States at club fed in Fort Walton Beach. Finally, being released after several years, he went back into the world and was never heard from again. The container that was shipped to Germany and then to the Middle East contained stuffed rabbits that looked like Peter Rabbit. When the container was opened, the terrorists, realizing what they had, ended up giving the stuffed animals to their kids.

John and Dan were transferred back to the United States to begin working as analysts, once their jobs were done in apprehending the terrorists. John would take care of the old woman for as long as she lived, and she was loved by John until she passed away years later. Her last words were, "Allah has truly blest me with a son."

Lucas and Miguel continued working for the FBI against the drug cartels in Mexico and South America. This all changed for Miguel and Lucas after their last adventure in Mexico City, working with Buck and Rachael.

Syria never could prove that Israel had anything to do with the destruction of the Scud missile site, and even if they could have proved it, who would blame the Israelis for destroying it? The loss of the MiG-21 was considered a shoot-down by the Syrian pilot, and he was treated as a hero for surviving the dog fight against the other MiG-21.

The terrorist group in Somalia was never able to recover from the damage done to them by the Seals and Mossad. Without their leader being there, they dwindled into being nothing but thugs for hire.

Sally liked working with Jennifer and found out that Jim had information on several key players in Washington. She joined the FBI to work with Jennifer and Bill not too long after graduating from Quantico as an agent.

Jim, who was sent to Gitmo, found his first love, the blonde, serving her time for being part of a terrorist cell in recruiting others to their cause.

www.ingramcontent.com/pod-product-compliance
Lightning Source LLC
Chambersburg PA
CBHW020803250626
47155CB00003B/1187